CW00450019

UNEXPECTED TALES

An Anthology of Short Stories from
authors living in three villages in
West Oxfordshire, England

First Published in 2017

ISBN 9781973337492

Introduction

In 2016, four of us gathered together ostensibly to taste wine, but it emerged over the course of the evening that we were all writing novels or short stories – or, in one person's case, just dreaming of doing so.

After reading each other's stories over subsequent weeks and realising that this spurred us on to greater discipline with our writing, we decided to go one step further ... well, several steps actually. After all, what would you expect if you put a police detective, a former journalist, a broadcast engineer and an ecologist together!

At the start of 2017, we announced our idea to produce an anthology of short stories from within our three villages of Freeland, Long Hanborough and North Leigh in Oxfordshire, not knowing who else might be affected by the area's water in a similar way. The residents did not disappoint, with a plethora of superb stories across many genres.

The result is this book ... and a slightly larger wine-tasting group.

So, is this the start of a series of short stories from these villages? We really don't know, but we can't resist a challenge and we certainly can't resist using a red pen on each other's work.

Regardless of whether we end up with an ongoing series of anthologies, if you have bought this book, you can rest assured that you will be supporting a good cause, because the profits made from the sale of this collection of short stories will be donated to a local children's hospice, Helen and Douglas House. This charity does invaluable work supporting terminally ill children, young adults and their families. More information about the charity can be found on their website: helenanddouglas.org.uk.

Finally, we would love to know your thoughts about the stories contained in this anthology. You can email us at: shortstoriesarefun@gmail.com

David, Martin, Matt and Steve
December 2017

Contents

A Big Fish - Khadija Rouf   1

The Stranger on Coffin Path - David Lawrence   13

The Lot of Gods - Martin Marais   31

La Accabadora e Las Roccas - Steven Battersby   55

The Wrath of Grapes - David Lloyd   73

The Thirty Year Rule - Matthew Coburn   89

Beyond the Barn - Stephen Young   103

Intolerance - David Lawrence   133

An Empty Nest - Rhonda Neal   151

A Second Chance - Lucy McGregor   165

A Team Player - Jackie Vickers   179

Outlaw's Trail to Nowhere - Martin Marais   191

The Essence of War is Secrecy - Thomas Begley   215

The Perfect Murder - Matthew Coburn   231

Contributors' Biographies   243

A Big Fish
Khadija Rouf

Oh God! He's seen me looking!

Millie hid behind her magazine quickly, feeling suddenly flushed. She feigned interest in an article entitled 'Top Ten Face Creams'. She'd grabbed the magazine at reception. Its glossy, satin pages slipped silently through her fingers as she leafed through the contents. She skimmed page after page of unsmiling females in stilted, angular poses. High end clothes on skeletal women, their kohl rimmed eyes looked hungrily back at her: heroin chic. Perfect reading material for a spa hotel.

Millie didn't dare raise her eyes to look at him.

She sipped her coffee, her hand shaking. She stared hard at the magazine. She held her breath. She listened intently to the tapping of cutlery on plates, the hum of voices and laughter.

A few moments passed. Nothing awful happened.

He hadn't come over and tapped her on the shoulder, demanding to know, *What the hell she was doing? Was she following him? How did she end up, so often, where he was*?

No, nothing awful happened. She breathed again, relieved. She wondered what on earth she was doing all this for; following a man around like some love-struck teenager, hiding behind magazines, diving into doorways, sinking low in the driver seat of her old car, for fear of being caught.

Her relief was short-lived. Deflation followed.

He'd met her before, but he didn't recognise her now.

She was obviously completely forgettable.

She felt compelled to look again, and nonchalantly lifted her head to look around the restaurant lounge.

He was no longer looking at her. He was reading *The Times* and drinking white wine, looking relaxed and wholly unconcerned. His hair was still slightly damp after his swim. He was handsome. There was no doubt about it. She found herself staring again, noticing the way the parquet floor reflected a honeyed glow onto his face. He was a George Clooney type, his black hair, flecked with silver. He was tall, with olive skin and green eyes. He'd taken care of himself; she imagined him playing sport, maybe tennis. Of course, he swam regularly, and she bet he went ski-ing too. He could have been a model. But, since he was blessed with intelligence, he'd gone into Law.

She watched him, patiently, discreetly. He blended so well with the paraphernalia of his world. Everything around him looked crisp, light and airy. There was an elegant spray of purple tulips in a creamy vase on his table. A lush green palm to his side softened and mottled the light around. The table cloth was starched linen, thick and inviting like a new bed sheet. His deep blue suit and yellow tie were a startling contrast to his surroundings.

He finished with the newspaper and diverted to his mobile. He scrolled through the messages on his phone before slipping it into his pocket.

He loosened his silk tie, took another sip of wine and looked at his watch. A waiter brought over his lunch; a slab of rare steak, crisp green salad and hunks of bread. He smiled at the waiter and then at the steak. He moved on to red wine.

Although she had waited patiently, Millie now felt dowdy and out of her depth. Her battered blue car was outside in the car park, surrounded by gleaming BMWs and Land Rovers. She'd looked at the menu, and ordered coffee, daunted by the cost of lunch and the fancy titles of the dishes. Her watch was high street, not designer.

She self-consciously smoothed down the lapels of her jacket. Last year's fashion.

Dejectedly, she couldn't help remembering her office conversation with Claire months before. Millie had been sitting at her desk, engrossed, studying his photograph. Thomas Pike.

"Ambitious, aren't you?"

Claire's voice had startled her. She'd felt herself stiffen and fumbled with the photo, putting it in her top drawer, urgently trying to look at her papers instead. She'd been embarrassed that Claire had caught her looking. Head bowed, pretending not to care, she'd tried to ignore her colleague's comment. The smell of Claire's cigarette smoke and cloying perfume wafted through the air.

"Never do things by halves, do you love?" she said, blowing smoke through her nostrils.

Millie coughed.

"Punching above your weight there, love," she said, perching herself on the edge of Millie's desk.

"I-I don't think you should be smoking in here, Claire," said Millie.

"What? Are you going to have me arrested?" Claire laughed.

Millie bit her lip. This had been Claire's territory before Millie had arrived on the scene.

"He's a big fish, love. He'll be quite a catch for someone. Not for you, though, girly. He's elusive. You think you have him and then he... swims away."

Millie had felt there was a sting in her words, not just meant for her. Claire had extinguished her cigarette in the remains of Millie's cup of coffee. There was a tiny hiss. "You don't mind, do you?" she asked.

But she didn't wait for Millie to answer. She'd finished her baiting. She smiled her thin, care-worn smile and slipped away.

Claire's comments played on Millie's mind. She should have stuck up for herself, but she didn't have sharp comebacks like Claire. Instead, things would churn in Millie's mind, and her retorts would take time to bubble to the surface. Always too late, long after the moment had passed.

And now Millie was wondering how she had got herself into this situation. She'd been spending more and more time following him around, nervously waiting and patiently hoping... until now she didn't even feel sure what she was waiting for. She swallowed hard and sipped her coffee again. It was getting cold and the bottom of her cup was coated in a sludgy mass of coffee grains.

Maybe I am crazy, she thought. *All these months of trying to get close to him. It's becoming unhealthy, obsessive.*

She knew that she should have got some perspective by now, but Claire's comments had only made her more determined, even if it was just to prove a point. She smoothed down the lapels on her jacket again and stared blankly at her magazine.

She remembered when she'd first met him.

"Thomas Pike," he'd said, smiling and holding out his hand. "But... call me Tom."

"Millie Jones," she'd said, shaking his hand. He was older than her, probably in his early forties. He had a dimple when he smiled. He had that easy air of someone sure of his own confidence. He filled the space around himself assuredly. He made people look at him.

She'd smiled back at him, feeling the world go a little out of kilter. Later, she'd looked at his hands as he tidied his papers. No wedding ring. It had been a brief meeting. He didn't remember her now. She supposed that she was nothing in his eyes.

Millie snapped out of her daydream. Something was wrong. A blonde woman had walked up to Thomas' table and was smiling at him. He stood up and pulled out a chair for her. She sat down. Millie felt her heart stop. She could hear the blood beating in her ears, drowning out the din of the restaurant.

Who the hell is she?

She was attractive, whoever she was. She had long blonde hair that snaked into beautiful curls. Blondey had the kind of glossy locks that film stars flaunted in adverts: *you're so worth it*! She crossed her legs, and a tantalising heel peeked from behind the table cloth. She wore skyscraper shoes that screamed money. This was a woman who could walk slowly to where she needed to go, and wherever she walked, it wouldn't be far. She uncoiled her lime green pashmina and draped it across the back of her chair.

Millie shifted in her seat and automatically tucked her feet under her chair. Her sensible court shoes made her feel about as classy as fish paste in the presence of caviar. She could feel her face flushing. *She wanted to know who this woman was and what she was saying to Thomas*. In all this time, there hadn't been a woman like her on the scene. *This could ruin everything*...

And then he leant across the table and kissed her. A brief,

sweet kiss. Both of them smiled, their lips glistening. They leaned into each other, like lovers, him twisting a lock of her hair around his fingers. He whispered something into her ear, and her eyes glittered. Millie felt flushed and angry, her heart banging against her rib cage.

He pulled back, still smiling. The waiter came back to clear Thomas's plate. The woman ordered something and the waiter went away again. Millie tried not to stare. She casually flicked through her magazine again, but her gaze kept darting back to them.

Then Thomas wasn't smiling anymore.

His hand discreetly reached into his jacket. What was he doing? What was he getting out of his pocket?

Millie held her breath. Thomas produced a small package from inside his jacket, from the breast pocket. The waiters bustled by, oblivious. Diners chatted, unaware. Millie felt her breath quicken. She put her hand flat against her chest, trying to slow her breathing. She smoothed down her lapels again, trying not to give herself away.

Surely, he wouldn't have the nerve? Here, in a public place? It's so obvious… but then, who'd suspect him here?

Blondey smiled. In fact, she beamed.

Thomas furtively slipped her the package. It was a small brown envelope. She quickly curled her long fingers around the envelope, and it disappeared into her clutch bag. Then, he was smiling again. They kissed again, briefly. The kind of kiss that makes people look and then quickly look

7

away, a very British custom.

But Millie couldn't help looking. *Perfect*, she thought. *Clever*. But then she mused on why, when he had so much going for him? And that smile was amazing. She caught her breath again.

But she had to put all that to one side now.

Millie gritted her teeth. Her instinct told her it was time to act. She had waited and waited so patiently all these months. She'd been waiting for some sign, some ripple in the waters, but he had been gliding through life untroubled, effortlessly. He'd left no trail. So finally, *this* was what she'd been waiting for.

They all had.

She grabbed at her lapel, urgently whispering, "He's passed a package, Sir. I'm making a move on him. Send back-up!"

She didn't wait to hear an answer from her superior. All these months, she had hoped that he would eventually slip up. She had worried that he'd realise he was under surveillance, that he would recognise her after their meeting on a case all that time ago.

Pike had been biding his time, being careful, keeping the waters around him crystal clear. He was cunning, she'd give him that.

Now, she'd got him!

Thomas Pike, successful lawyer; handsome, charming and confident. Regularly down at Headquarters on some drugs case or another. And all the time, he was as corrupt as the criminals he was helping to prosecute. Well, it was one way to get rid of the competition. She needed to remember that right now.

She stood up, the glossy magazine falling onto the parquet. She bounded over to his table, pulling out her badge. She held it high, so there could be no doubt about who she was. Thomas and the woman looked at her, curiously at first. Then realisation spread across their faces. The blonde woman looked alarmed, and pulling her arms away from Thomas, knocked his glass of red wine across the linen. It spread like a blood stain. The other diners stopped eating and talking. They watched events unfolding in shocked silence.

"I'm Detective Constable Millie Jones. Thomas Pike, I'm arresting you for the possession of drugs with intent to supply."

Pike and the woman looked shocked, their mouths hanging open. Millie knew her gut instincts had been right. She pointed at Blondey's clutch bag.

"Please empty your bag, Miss."

The woman looked ashen, and looked at Thomas helplessly. He nodded slowly. The woman extracted the envelope. Inside, there was a thick wad of cash, and some small white packages, wrapped in plastic. She looked at Pike and the woman. She felt flushed, elated.

"You do not have to say anything. But it may harm your

defence if you do not mention, when questioned, something you later rely on in court. Anything you do say may be given in evidence," she said, fired with adrenaline. "Do you have anything you wish to say?"

His eyes were wide. For a second he looked like he was going to run. But something quickly shifted in his expression, and he just shook his head.

"Of course, you know your rights, don't you, Mr Pike?" she said.

She knew that he didn't remember their previous meeting. He wouldn't forget her this time.

Other officers were arriving now. The other customers in the restaurant began murmuring to each other, and some dabbed their lips with their napkins and went to the reception desk so they could settle their bills quickly. People stared at Pike as he stood up slowly. The blonde woman looked at him, her face pale and fearful. "Tom?" she asked.

He didn't answer.

Millie felt a pang as she watched him being handcuffed.

"Please mind my watch," he said. "It's very expensive."

He looked at her with his aquamarine eyes; a look which was filled with bewilderment. He suddenly looked like a lost boy.

Millie looked away, trying to break his spell.

In the eerie quiet, Millie's elation with catching Pike was fractured by the realisation that she had become obsessed with him. Other officers were speaking to him now. She looked at the handcuffs around his wrists, large metallic bands. She looked again at those hands, no wedding ring. Her heart was thudding.

She brushed away an uncomfortable thought; that there would now be a hole where he had been. She had lived this case in detail; got to know him, how he dressed, how he spent his time, where he went. She had been told to learn to think like him, to the point where she might even anticipate his decisions.

She'd seen him every day for months and now it was over.

She caught her breath. *No,* she wanted to catch predators like him. Underneath all that fine talk and confidence and supposedly good breeding, he was someone who had decided to dwell in murky waters. He fed off the miserable addiction of others. They got hooked in, and then they would spiral down, down, until they vanished. Tom Pike was deplorable, because he'd had all the advantages life could offer. He had no excuses.

She walked outside into the car park, and watched Pike being put into the back of a police car. He looked at her through the glass, before the car sped away. He looked like he was underwater. *He knows,* she thought, *he knows he's going down for a very long time. His career is finished.*

As Millie walked towards her old, unmarked police car, she made herself think about Claire. She remembered

Claire sitting in the office, blowing cigarette smoke into her face and extinguishing her cigarette butt in Millie's coffee. She remembered the small hissing sound, and her inability to say anything back to her colleague. Claire had resented Millie being assigned to the case. She had mocked her that day, as Millie was intently studying the file and Thomas Pike's photograph.

Punching above your weight there, love, she'd said.

He's a big fish, she'd said.

Well, it wouldn't hurt to walk into Headquarters having bagged her man.

No, that wouldn't hurt at all, because Claire was right.

He was quite a catch.

The Stranger on Coffin Path

David Lawrence

'You don't know me. You'll hope it stays that way. Everything set down here is the absolute truth. Whether you judge me or find these events less than plausible is of little concern to me. How literal you believe the truth to be is up to you. I know what I did and I know what I saw. Is it allegory? Is it a fantasy? It's neither. It's the truth.'

This was the introduction on the flysheet of a manuscript I uncovered during one of my research trips to the Bodleian library. I had spent most of the morning in the new Weston Library in Broad Street before crossing over to the Radcliffe Camera to look through a number of old liturgical texts relating to the West Oxfordshire diocese, when the above statement caught my eye. It seemed so…decisive.

What I have reproduced for you here is the text I then sat and read. I have rendered it as far as possible into a more contemporary style. I cannot say how it got here or who originally wrote it down. What agents conspired to put these words in front of me I cannot say. Given the context, it is unlikely that it was the narrator who put pen to paper.

I am Robert Walters, Rector of Longhandboro, at least that is the name that comes most readily to mind. Given my perilous state I cannot be certain. Perhaps history knows me by another name. Either way my tale is a cautionary one you would do well to take seriously. I am or was a man of God, but my tale has very little to do with Him and more to do with Man. This man.

It begins in the summer of 1644, during my forty-fifth year. I had completed some church business and was on my way to meet one of my older parishioners. I heard the church strike five as I hurried along the Coffin Path that connects the parish church and the main village about a mile away. For several hundred years, it had been the final route travelled by parishioners on their way for burial in the grounds of the church. The funereal route took a south-easterly course through common land, from the long elevated part of the village before skirting the western perimeter of Pinsley Wood. The path, well worn by generations of mourners, eventually joins a narrow lane leading to the tall imposing spire of the Church of St Peter and St Paul.

I was walking north west from the church. The air was fresh and warm; alive to the wind rippling the long grasses and wild flowers that graced the lovely idyll between the two halves of the village. During the day, Coffin Path, despite its name, was a charming place, a part of the earth that can invigorate the bleakest of souls. But when night fell it seemed to teem with voices so that the superstitious and the recently bereaved would never set foot on it, which in those days was nearly everyone.

And there I was, lost in my own thoughts regarding some unsettling business within the Bishopric and the Deacons of St John's College in particular. My parish fell within the influence of St John's so I was effectively their man. Despite the vigour of my pace and the enriching fragrance of wild flowers in deep grass, the mesmerising hum of bees and the eye-catching grace of white admirals, my mood had become dark and unchristian. With my eyes to the ground and my head covered by a black cowl, I must have struck a doleful figure. In truth, my soul had become consumed by self-pity.

I first saw him when the path took me close to the ancient wood of Pinsley. The main carpet of bluebells had gone over but there was still much to admire in the many shades of green and the ash and elms standing proud at the borders of this ancient woodland. I was struck by the sound of jackdaws fussing in the long grass under the outer eaves, and a murder of crows cawing loudly in the treetops as they fought for territory. One large bird, almost the size of a raven, came down from its roost and broke my reverie. Its sudden approach was startling. Huge frantic wings beat hard and brushed my face as it came too close before soaring away. I watched its judgemental eyes staring back, unblinking, before I lost it in the low rays of the sun. A shadow crossed my path and the stranger was at my elbow.

He was a tall, lean man perhaps thirty years old who spoke first, apologising for startling me. He said that his name was Captain Jack and wondered whether he could accompany me up to the village. His brogue was local, perhaps more rural than city. He said that he was a soldier cut off from his regiment and he was a man of the people, which I'm not sure I fully understood. To my untrained eye, his clothes were from a previous era. His jerkin and side-arms, a long rapier and a dirk, were more Tudor or even Plantagenet. This was not entirely unheard of. When country folk take to soldiering, they are often forced to borrow their weaponry from old soldiers in the family.

He fell in step, seemingly oblivious of my mood, but after a while I was glad of the company, which I hoped would clear my mind and lighten my brooding disposition. He was a friendly fellow and, although he didn't seem to have been formally educated, he was one of those men who, if life had dealt a kinder hand, would have made more of a fierce intellect. We spoke on a range of topics. Good and evil, the church, the monarchy and justice. It was all quite pertinent, deep as we were in the grip of civil war.

His knowledge of older conflicts was strong which gave our conversation an historical perspective. He talked in detail about the Lancaster and York War some 160 years or so before, which I called the War of the Roses, a phrase he didn't recognise. We agreed that men were unique in their capacity to learn but equally unique when they steadfastly refused to. It was as if the species was cursed with a sort of divine madness. He said there was always another way to avoid bloodshed, if men would just shed their pride instead. He thought that all men got what they deserved in the end, which I said was a central theme of many faiths although we also have the capacity to forgive. He nodded and said no more on the subject. As I said, he was a bright fellow.

We came at last to the wide dirt road, a thoroughfare carrying traffic from the capital (the old capital of London that is) into the west. It forded streams and rivers, linked ancient trails and green roads before crossing the Cotswolds and on towards the Marches. The turmoil and thunder of civil war was tearing the country apart, setting neighbour against neighbour, brother against brother and father against son. Storm clouds were gathering now that the King had moved his court to Oxford. The war had raged all around the county, but the village had remained largely unscathed. The sight of Royalist armies passing through was not unknown but every day the threat of Cromwell's New Model Army coming closer meant that the people lived in a state of perpetual anxiety.

We turned west into the village itself, following the route taken the previous evening by the Royalist Army; many thousands of horsemen were now camped upon Hanboro Heath in front of Abel Wood. The King was moving his forces west. The villagers, alert to the stir and noise of the passing army, had come out to cheer and to swear allegiance to their monarch. The king, they said, for I was not there, struck a proud, aloof figure, who nevertheless had the good grace to acknowledge the good wishes of his people.

The locals were, by this time, making their ways home. The women carrying baskets from the single shop on the main road, that was both grocer and butcher, and the men coming off the land in twos or threes. A cart passed us filled with farming equipment and a coach was fast approaching bound for Woodstock and then Oxford. We stepped aside as it rushed passed, scattering chickens and dogs scavenging on the dirt road.

The Captain observed that the people seemed civil enough to me, but there was, he thought, some tension. I was unwilling to explain, at least for the moment. My companion had not said where he was going exactly, but I explained that I had someone to meet, so I stopped to wish him well before moving on. But he was a persuasive fellow and asked whether I would join him for supper. I should really have carried on to see the widow I was hoping to comfort in her hour of need but the thought of a more companionable evening and the chance to drown out the voices in my head weakened my resolve. I said I would.

He asked me where we should go and I suggested we turned about and retrace our steps. So we walked back along the main road, past the end of Coffin Path and on towards the Katherine Wheel set back on the left, some 200 yards from the Manor House that loomed further along on the south side of the road. The inn's chimney leaned out at an unfeasible angle from an unkempt thatched roof, above dusty white-washed walls and large leaded windows. Thick smoke billowed up, caught on the breeze that blew perpetually through the village. The smell of rich gravy and cooked meat drew us on. The Inn was weathered, rambling, but welcoming.

A solid door, made of good local oak felled on the estates in Woodstock, was ajar and we pushed our way in. The Katherine Wheel had gained a certain notoriety as an ill-kept hostelry attracting all kinds of ne'er-do-wells and footpads who, in the grip of the strongest ale in the county, would usually succumb before the night was out to illegal trading, gambling, fisticuffs or worse. Despite this, it provided a respite for the yeomen of the Manor. After a long day labouring in the fields or the brick kilns further west, weary bodies would make their way here, looking for fellowship. Most would be back out on the land before dawn.

Old Joseph was a genial landlord providing the very finest ales and supper cooked by his wife, Nell. It was the only inn in the village and also the oldest surviving as others had come and gone, usually owned by folk opening up their front parlour with a few kegs before shutting down again once they had sold out.

The low-beamed bar was dim but lively. Drink-fuelled characters were talking loudly over each other or sitting in morose silence, their bones aching. The evenings that summer had been considerably cooler than was seasonal. Old Joe had lit the log fire in the inglenook. We were greeted by nodding heads and 'Good evening father' by members of the flock I had tended these past ten years. More than a few did not appear to see me or averted their gaze as I approached. But I knew that I had done the right thing. I needed something to push back this melancholia.

It was here that the seeds of my doom were sown. I set up a few rounds of local ale, strong dark liquid that loosens the tongue or confines a man to reflective silence. We ordered steak and kidney pudding, which is the specialty of the landlord's wife, and we ate heartily until we sat back and Captain Jack took out a pipe and filled it from a pouch on his belt. I took the moment to enquire after his regiment and his part in the war and he said that he was an old soldier despite his looks. His swarthy complexion, deep expressive eyes, patriarchal brow and generous mouth suggested a certain nobility, but there was pain in his eyes that he failed to completely hide.

Captain Jack enquired after my constitution, by which he meant my allegiance. I said that I was a patriot like him and God fearing, which made him smile. He drew deep on his smoke and it seemed as though he could see into my heart. It was probably the ale, but I said far more than I intended. I was a man of the people, like him, and I wished that the country would be rid of the scourge of monarchy. It was reckless talk and my companion urged me to keep my voice down. He was right. In those days, there were eyes and ears everywhere. Nevertheless, it was no surprise that he shared this view for his dress said something of the common man. He said that this explained the strained relationship I appeared to have with my Royalist flock.

People in Longhandboro hardly spoke of the war, preferring instead to tend their farms and crops, be neighbourly and spend their time pursuing the finer things in life. My companion asked about my position within the parish, which I found curious given the prospect of my removal, but I was too much in my cups to resist. It was as if he was inviting me to unburden my soul, to confess even.

I welcomed the opportunity to talk about the events eating away at me. Much like the country, my mind was ruptured by competing forces. Thanks to the war, there had been a great deal of debate at St John's College concerning the suitability of a man like me remaining in a position of such influence. My affiliations with the people, the traitorous Cromwell as they put it, put me at odds with the king's appointed bishop, especially now that his See was the new military capital. It was put plainly. I should renounce my allegiance or step down and move out of the city. If I wished to continue my pastoral work then I should consider a monastery or, better still, go abroad. They considered their offer generous given that trial and excommunication were well within their gift. But I would not stand aside and fell into a miasma of bitterness and deep self-loathing that surprised me. My thoughts became disparate and unfocused like flotsam tossed this way and that until the frailties in my soul were exposed. Even prayer provided little in the way of solace.

"I was turning this over when you found me."

Like a child, I fixed my gaze on the Captain, hoping he would offer some sort respite.

"Tell me, Father," he said at last, "have you reached a decision?"

I looked at him, unable to answer, because honestly I had reached the end of my tether. He continued, sensing my despair.

"Will you let them take your job after... how long?"

"Ten years..."

"... ten years as their shepherd? Are you able to swallow your pride, to leave your flock and do as they say, perhaps until the war is won... or lost?"

"That's just it, Captain. I can neither change nor leave."

Captain Jack puffed away serenely. The tobacco seemed to bring him a calm release from whatever was causing him pain. An epiphany had been reached. His dark eyes examined me as I stared blankly back, hoping that he would say something to help me. I was all but pleading.

"Are there really only two alternatives?" he offered.

I waited for more.

"Perhaps there is another way of approaching this – a way to cut the Gordian Knot, as they say."

He pressed on.

"What is the cause of your dilemma? The root cause I mean."

"The church and the monarchy," I said without hesitation. He nodded his understanding.

"And of these two?"

"The monarchy." Without their arrogance and bloated sense of self-worth, my relationship with the church would be unchanged. I was a pastor who held faith to be of greater worth than the rules of state. Like St Paul, I was a true servant of God, and not one of the hypocrites he so despised, who confused the law with faith.

"And if this could be resolved at a stroke? Would you?"

"Of course... but how?"

"What would you be willing to do?"

The captain had become bold, which I welcomed. He was encouraging me to think the unthinkable. I glanced around the inn as if my inner thoughts were suddenly exposed. I summoned my courage like a man staring directly into the sun knowing that where the light is too bright, blindness may follow. But I was emboldened and sensed a path to salvation.

"Anything. I think I would do anything to maintain my position."

"Your position? What of the people's position?"

"Of course, it would be for the people."

He took the pipe from his lips and chuckled, I think to

himself, as if I wasn't there.

"And you a man of God," he said and smiled in a way that made his eyes flash and the fire in the grate flare up. In that moment I saw the four men sat apart in a discrete inglenook, wrapped in black cloaks despite the season and the fire. Captain Jack leaned in conspiratorially.

"Those gentlemen," he jabbed his pipe stem in their direction, "are king's men. The one at the back smoking the clay pipe. Do you see him?"

A man in the deepest shadows blew elaborate smoke rings across the table as his companions spoke in hushed voices, his devilishly handsome face occasionally illuminated by the crackling fire.

"He…" began Captain Jack, "he is…"

"Prince Rupert of the Rhine, my God," I had seen this peacock before in the city but never at such close quarters, and never so discreet.

"But why here?" I wondered out loud.

"There were no horses outside," said the Captain, "so they are probably at the smithy. If they are waiting to collect them, what better way to pass the time than to come here and relax, safe in royalist country. I've no doubt they will head for the Heath before long."

One of their number looked our way and raised a tankard to me. I reciprocated but couldn't help wonder what he made of my drinking companion who looked for all the world a Parliamentarian. It was as if he only saw me. I watched them speaking and occasionally laughing. They were a tight group, comfortable in each other's company. When the Prince spoke it was to the rapt attention of the others, who I reasoned were not bodyguards, but high ranking officers spending time with a commander they respected.

The rest of the evening passed very slowly and my thoughts began to whirl. I was becoming a new man, productive and ready to do God's work once more. My black mood had become a cocktail of euphoria and anger, and it drove my tormented soul out into the light. There had been a long black river blocking my way, but I had glimpsed a bridge to the other side. Whether it was the strong dark ale or the Captain's words I don't know, but by the time the messenger came I had completely forgotten Widow Brown and was on my mettle.

The four king's men drank up, and rose like great bats, throwing long inky shadows across the flagstone floor. I felt a surge of fear and something else, something unfamiliar.

"What would you be willing to do?"

"Anything... ."

The words were ringing loud and clear through my head until I feared once more that they would echo through the inn for all the world to hear. Then it became the voice of certainty, rejoicing in its sense of purpose. But, despite my raised spirit, I had not grasped the profundity of what was happening until Captain Jack pushed a long dagger into my hand. It was the dirk that had been in his belt. I flinched at the touch of cold steel.

"Here is the king's own beloved nephew, the apple of his eye and the ablest general in the royalist army," he hissed. "As long as he lives there can be no victory for Cromwell or the people, or men of faith like you."

I was speechless.

"We are blessed Father. There will never be a moment like it. Look at him. Cocksure no one can harm him. The people, the honest ones you represent, will never have an opportunity like this again. Do not let this cup pass. He is yours."

I instinctively recoiled from the knife. No one appeared to have seen the gesture and my skin crawled with cold sweat.

"But… why me… why not you? You are the soldier."

He puffed confidently as he answered.

"They would not allow me near enough but you… a man of the cloth… you have the perfect disguise."

"This is no disguise…"

"Isn't it?"

We watched the four officers leave and, as they passed, I heard Prince Rupert laugh at something one of them said. To my heightened senses he was laughing at all good men of faith. He was mocking men like me. He was laughing at me! They were over-confident, arrogant even. Men nodded respectfully as they went.

Captain Jack put the dagger hilt back into my hand beneath the table. This time, to my own shame, I felt my fingers grip the cold wooden handle and take it from him. I concealed the blade beneath my robes and sat back to watch the rest of the room, the characterful faces, the innocent conversation, the furtive glances at Nell and the bonhomie of villagers at rest. And I wondered how it had come to this, to be so alone. By the grace of God I could still walk away. It would be so easy to say what they wanted, to swear allegiance to the king and his brood. Who would know? What was holding me back? I didn't have to mean it, after all God would still know my heart. But I was a man of principle.

I rose unsteadily to my feet and waited while the Captain allowed himself a few seconds to finish his ale and to extinguish his pipe, knocking the tobacco noisily onto the floor. He seemed assured, languid and relaxed. He got to his feet and followed me out into the warm evening air. The village was all but asleep as we made our way along the road a few yards behind the four cavaliers who swaggered along roaring and laughing to each other. A rich canopy of stars hung over the village as if the world was a secret place known only to we few out on the road that night. The moonlight cast silver beams across the thatched roofs throwing the fields beyond into black relief and giving the road itself a glow as if it were faerie.

The Captain and I trailed the Prince, keeping a suitable

distance to avoid suspicion. But the Captain had been right, who would suspect a man of the cloth? Then one of the officers turned.

"Good evening, Father," he said, a Colonel I suspected, "may we accompany you? These are strange and troublesome times to be out alone."

All four of them waited until I had caught them up. In their company I could see they were well appointed men of wealth, dressed in cloaks and silks, and they wore their hair long as was the fashion of their class. The fragrance of rose-water or something similar was in the air.

And so I fell in with Prince Rupert and his three officers as they strolled to the smithy at the edge of the village where a lane turned north toward Mill Wood. They asked what brought me onto the road at such an hour and I told them about Widow Brown who lived at the Rows further ahead. Their spirits in the grip of good Oxfordshire ale had turned them into a gay group, but my heart remained as unmoved as stone. I noted that the Captain hung back, keeping to the shadows of the cottages and trees. I was sure that my companions had not seen him.

I offered them my gratitude and they confirmed that the Prince was having two new shoes put onto his charger at the forge where they had temporarily stabled the others. It was their intention to re-join the king before riding at dawn towards Gloucester. The Prince himself seemed reluctant to engage in conversation, but nodded and said good evening.

He smiled the smile of a man used to courtly etiquette, but his eyes were those of a man more used to demanding and getting his own way. In short, close up, I could see that Prince Rupert was no fop, but a man not to be trifled with. I must admit my nerve wavered as we exchanged pleasantries.

We came to the junction with a lane that ran south toward the Church. Ahead I could hear the smith readying their horses and I heard barking too. The Prince turned to me in delight and said that was his faithful poodle, Boy, who had kept his horse company. I felt myself warming to the man and knew the deed had to be done before my nerve failed altogether.

At the junction I could feel fire raging in my skull, a ferment of oil and flames destroying all rational thought. I was sweating which forced me to grip the knife tighter for fear of dropping it. I saw indistinct shapes moving either side of me, their voices lost in a low murmur. All reason left me. I glanced back at the Captain who nodded and I pulled the knife from my cloak and hurled myself at Prince Rupert's back.

Moonlight flashed on steel as I swung the blade down. But these were trained fighters, men of some renown. Rapiers were drawn and I was cut down and run through more than once. I dropped the knife and fell on my knees in the dust before suffering another blade through my chest. The final cut. In the light of the fierce unforgiving moon the last thing I saw was Captain Jack laughing as he shrank back into the shadows. I fell face down in the road and lay still.

My eyes opened to a kind of half-light and I became aware of my fate. It is now me, not Captain Jack, who walks beneath the eaves of Pinsley Wood. As a betrayer of all that is holy, my soul stands cursed and alone among the jackdaws and the crows. I never knew what crime Captain Jack had committed or how long he had been trapped in the woods, but his soul had found peace at last. Now it is my sins that keep me chained to this mortal earth, unable to live or die. I accompany the dead on their way to their final resting place. We walk and we talk, but in the end they always leave me. As for the living, my only hope for peace is to inflame the black heart of a passerby and lead them where they should not go. Only then will I enjoy salvation and release. So beware my friends, if ever you come this way; I shall be here watching and waiting.

The Lot of Gods

Martin Marais

"And that," Isokrates concluded dramatically, his eyes scanning the awed faces of his audience, "is how I got the scar."

As he stood up, the gloomy light of the tavern's tallow lanterns seemed to realign and focus on him. He lifted his tattered tunic and turned. One of the shepherds, who was sat at the table, raised a lamp to allow a better view and the rest of them gathered around to examine the scar. Of course, they had seen it before, but as, undoubtedly, the most courageous shepherd amongst them, Isokrates received their utmost respect and they went through the well-established ritual. Some could not resist, but to hover their fingers down the lengths of the ragged claw marks that the bear had left etched on Isokrates' back. None, however, dared touch them.

Old Kleitos, who alone had remained seated, smiled to himself as he watched the men go through the ritual. They had all heard the story before, many times, but it was a magnificent story, the best of them all. Isokrates was a past master at telling tales, which was why his story was always the last to be told during the shepherds' gatherings on these cold winter nights. Kleitos lifted his leather tankard and took a draught of his warm mead. He was the oldest shepherd in the valley, by far, and his great age and infirmity excused him from the ceremony of examining the scar.

The men settled down and, with the story-telling over, they gathered into twos and threes to discuss the more mundane matters that beset the life of a shepherd in the Caucasus.

Kleitos felt a small flutter in his chest and then that breathless feeling that he now got whenever he walked any distance. He grasped the edge of the table tightly with both hands and waited for the discomfort to pass. Meliton, sitting beside him, saw the look of fear in the old man's eyes. He went to aid his aged mentor, but Kleitos raised spread fingers to stop him. Meliton stayed where he was, but kept a keen eye on his ancient mentor. Kleitos closed his eyes and listened as the murmur of his life-long friends rolled over him like warm water. He slowed his breathing. He relaxed his body. His heart steadied. After a moment he looked at Meliton and smiled.

"It has passed."

Meliton breathed a sigh of relief. He smiled at the old man.

Kleitos let his eyes roam over the other shepherds. None were of his generation. He was the last of his cohort. These young men were brave, but brash, living the modern way. Living life to the full for, although life was peaceful at present, no-one ever knew when they would be called upon to fight some devastating war against some foe or other. And with the cities of Sparta, Argos, Corinth and Athens, amongst others, all vying for power, another war seemed inevitable. He was pleased he was too old to be involved. He had had a good life, an ordinary life, except for that one event. He gazed at Meliton. It was something about which he and Meliton had never spoken – something that still gave him nightmares, some forty winters later. He rubbed his chest soothingly. Maybe his time was near. If it was, then now would be the time to tell the story of the scars he had kept hidden for all this time.

He took his leather tankard and drank it dry. Meliton looked at him in surprise; the old man was normally a cautious drinker. Kleitos banged his jug onto the table. The younger men jumped and then fell into respectful silence.

Kleitos held Meliton's gaze and said, "I have a tale to tell."

Meliton's eyes widened in surprise. He gave the minutest shake of his head.

"It is time," said Kleitos, smiling at his younger friend.

"Now old man," Isokrates said playfully, "we have already heard how you chased the wolf, throwing stones at it and how you tripped and scarred your knee."

The others laughed heartily.

Kleitos smiled. "That story was made up. I tell it to amuse you. It sets the story telling sessions off to a good start. You may believe I have had a very ordinary life. And, on the whole, I have. I certainly have not fought off a bear, but I have fought an eagle. It was an incident that happened to me, and to Meliton, many seasons ago. Meliton was still my apprentice then, that is how long ago it was, but I remember it as if it were only yesterday. It is a tale about which we have never spoken a word to anyone. We were, indeed, on the trail of a wolf that had been taking our sheep. We had tracked it to the upper slopes of Mount Ararat, and it is a story that will turn your blood to ice."

He now had the full attention of all the shepherds. He lifted his tankard and took a long sip; it was for effect – the vessel was empty. He looked over its rim at his attentive audience. He placed the tankard on the scratched table and settled into the hard, wooden seat and said reflectively, as if to himself, "I remember it like it happened only yesterday."

*

Meliton and I had been chasing the wolf for hours and I was starting to wonder about the futility of the hunt.

"Bloody hell, Meliton," I cursed, "where in the name of the gods are you taking us? If we carry on any further we'll end up in Tartarus itself."

I saw Meliton give the sign of self-preservation at the mention of the underworld. "Don't make those sorts of jokes, Master. It's Brutus," he said, pointing at my wolfhound. "He's onto something. He's following the scent of the wolf, I'm sure of it."

"Brutus is a good sheepdog," I called back. "Probably the best dog I've ever had. He's certainly the bravest, but this is ridiculous. We started just before day-break and now the sun is almost at its zenith. We have been following this wolf for hours. It does not make sense that it would take our sheep and bring them this far up the mountain."

"Look," Meliton pointed. "Look at Brutus!"

"He certainly looks troubled," I noted.

The dog had stopped at a point where the mountain track rounded an outcrop of black rock. The hackles of his grey coat were raised, making him look twice his normal size. His black lips were curled back and he bared his ivory teeth as a low growl rumbled from his throat. Meliton set a stone into his sling and I gripped my staff more tightly. Brutus slunk forward, his heavy shoulders rolling slowly as he advanced cautiously around the outcrop. Meliton followed, his sling whirring through the cold mountain air. I followed along the narrow, stony track, my staff twitching in anticipation of what we would see around the corner.

As we edged our way along the path it widened into a small, flat shelf of rock perched on the side of the mountain. In the centre of the shelf there was a single block of black granite. It was about seven feet in length and four feet in width, with a surface as smooth as a mill pond. It looked like an altar. It was inclined slightly along its length and the upper surface shone as if covered by a veneer of some dark, lustrous material. Heavy chains looped here and there across and around the smooth surface of the rock. They glistened in the dull light of the cloudy sky.

Brutus edged forward aggressively, his growl rising in pitch as he moved towards something huddled at the base of the altar-like stone. It looked like a pile of rags, and seemed to be the point from which the chain links originated. The growl in Brutus' throat died away, he slunk up to the filthy rags and gave them a cautious sniff. The rags stirred, the chain clicked and Brutus leapt back, barking angrily. The rags jerked as if in surprise as Brutus' barking echoed noisily around the crags of the mountain. It was a man, although he looked more like some feral beast than anything that might be described as human. He stared at Brutus with wild eyes, but his face showed no fear. Then his eyes flitted towards Meliton and myself. He studied us slowly, with keen eyes that were sunken within the sockets of his gaunt, bearded face. He uncurled from his slumbering position and sat up. The front of his shirt was torn into strips and heavily stained with old blood, although there seemed to be no wounds from which any blood could have flowed. He leant back against the smooth side of the altar block and continued to scrutinise us with interest. We remained transfixed to the spot. When he spoke, his voice was hoarse, as though his throat pained him, like it might do if you screamed and screamed until your throat seared with agony.

"Why are you here?" he rasped.

I dipped my head respectfully at him, for, although he looked like the rawest beggar, his countenance seemed to demand veneration. "We are hunting a wolf, My Lord. It has been taking our sheep."

"It has not passed this way. Nothing has passed this way for eons. You are the first living beings, other than the eagle, that I have seen since I was placed here. What are your names?"

"I… I am… Kleitos, and this is my apprentice, Meliton," I stammered.

"And you are shepherds."

I nodded.

"Then I suggest you leave, before it is too late."

I took a step forward. "Before it is too late for what, My Lord."

"You do not wish to know."

I walked towards him and dropped to my knees before him so I could study the gaunt features. They seemed out of place with the smooth, muscular torso and his obviously strong arms and legs. His eyes were dark brown and bright, but there was a resignation within their depths.

"Is there anything that we can do to help? Do you need food, water?"

He laughed at my comment. "I get all the food and refreshment I require. More than I need." He pulled some of his rags aside to reveal a golden platter piled with the most glorious meats and fruits imaginable. Beside the platter was a small flagon of wine and a golden goblet. "Are you hungry?"

I nodded before I could stop myself. My mouth was watering at the sight of the food. I had never seen such appetising food in all my life.

"Help yourself."

His tone was irresistible. It was as if he was able to control our actions and we both set about consuming the delicious victuals. I am no expert in the matters of wine, but if all wine is like that which we had that day, then I could live on it and nothing else – if I had the where-with-all, which unfortunately I do not. It ran down one's throat like satin.

The man watched us eat, as though we amused him.

I flushed with embarrassment. "We eat your food and yet we do not even know the name of our generous host."

He laughed lightly. "I am called Prometheus."

Meliton leapt to his feet and away from the Titan in shock. I fell onto my back in my haste to get away from the god. If we were transfixed before, we were now paralysed with fear. I lay where I had fallen, unable to move. In my peripheral vision, I could see Meliton shaking and bobbing his head and uttering little sounds of distress as if he were a simpleton.

Prometheus laughed at our reaction. "Finish eating and then leave," he said softly.

His warm tones banished the fear that had gripped my

heart. And, watching him cautiously, I resumed drinking and eating. Meliton came and squatted beside me and cautiously took some food.

"Thank you, My Lord," he said, in an awestruck tone.

Avoiding looking directly at the god I asked, "Why are you in chains, My Lord? Surely, being a god, you can break free."

Prometheus laughed at my ignorance. "I am bound here by Zeus. No man, mortal or immortal, can break the binds set by Zeus. Except maybe one; and he is not here."

"May I ask another question, My Lord?"

"You may."

"Why did Zeus bind you to this rock?"

"You query the will of the gods?" he stormed, although I sensed some amusement, behind his anger.

I dropped my head instantly. "No, My Lord. Please forgive my insolence."

"Look at me," he ordered.

I slowly raised my head, expecting to be struck down for my disrespect, but behind the beard he was smiling. His eyes sparkled with mirth.

"Do you wish to hear my story?"

"Only if My Lord wishes to tell it," I said quickly.

He looked up and scanned the sky momentarily. "I have time," he declared. He settled into a more comfortable position against the rock and held his hand out for the goblet. I passed it to him, reverentially. He took a small sip, filled it and passed it back to me.

"You have heard of the Titanomachy?"

I nodded.

Meliton's nod was less certain. "I have heard of it, but I am uncertain what it is," he admitted.

Prometheus looked at him. "It is important you understand, because it is our history that sets the path of our destiny."

*

"The Titanomachy," Prometheus said, "was the great war between the Titans, the old gods, and the Olympians, the gods who now rule. It lasted for ten terrible years. The ruler and commander of the Titans was Cronus. The Olympians were commanded by Zeus, the youngest son of Cronus.

"Before Cronus came to rule the Titans, the gods were ruled by his father Uranus. But Uranus was a tyrant and Cronus deposed him. The years that followed were known as the Golden Age. It was a time when there was no need for laws or rules. Everyone did what was right. They lived lives of respect for others and of humility. Immorality and jealously did not exist.

"But then Cronus learnt, from a seer, that he would be deposed by his sons in the same manner in which he had usurped rule from his own father. He became corrupted by the fear of losing control and the world was plunged into darkness. He devoured his new-born sons so that they could not rise up against him. But Rhea, his wife, hid their youngest son, Zeus, and when he came of age, Zeus rose up against his father, and so began the Titanomachy.

"Disgusted by the tyranny of Cronus, I sided with my cousin, Zeus, and after ten terrible years, Zeus and his Olympians were victorious." Prometheus paused and looked at Meliton. "You have a question?"

Meliton nodded. "You fought for Zeus, and yet he still bound you to this rock? I do not understand."

"You will in due course," Prometheus responded grimly. "Immediately after his victory Zeus was virtuous and benevolent. But, as with all who gain power, he started to demand recognition from those over whom he ruled. The focus of his arrogance was not on the gods, but on the mortals. He started to demand sacrifices. Initially, he demanded only small, insubstantial offerings, but as his arrogance grew he demanded more and more by way of offerings. Eventually the priests requested a meeting with the gods to discuss what would fulfil the requirements of Zeus and be acceptable to the mortals. The meeting took place in the city of Mecone." Prometheus paused, and looked again at Meliton. "You have heard about this?"

Meliton nodded. "I have, My Lord."

"Then tell me what you know."

Meliton gulped. He hoped he would get the story correct. "I believe, My Lord, it goes something like this. Zeus and his entourage, including yourself, My Lord, met the priests at Mecone, the city we now call Sicyon. There was much heated debate. It is said that Zeus took the opportunity to try and increase the size and value of the sacrifices he wished to be made to him. The priests, of course, tried to make him see reason, but it was clear that they were unlikely to win the argument. And then you, My Lord, intervened, although I do not understand why a god would take the side of mere mortals."

"I did so," Prometheus said, "because I could see Zeus going the same way as his father Cronus. Power had gone to his head and there was the danger of him turning into a tyrant, as his father had."

Meliton bowed his head at the god. "We are indebted to you, My Lord."

"Carry on with the story," Prometheus commanded.

"During the debate, you asked for an ox to be brought into the room. You stipulated it had to be the largest beast available and the most magnificent in terms of power and horns. Such a beast was found and brought to you. You then told everyone, including Zeus and his entourage, to leave the room. After a while you requested everyone return to the room and they saw that you had slaughtered the ox and made two piles of its remains. One pile seemed to consist of the stomach and intestines. The other, larger pile was covered in a layer of glistening fat. It is said that Zeus' gaze fell immediately on the larger pile. Once everyone was back in their place, with Zeus back on his throne, you stood before him, saying, 'My Lord, I have slaughtered the beast and from it I have made two sacrifices to you. I wish you to decide which offering you are to accept.'

"Zeus immediately went to choose the larger, more appealing looking pile, but you held up your hand to forestall him, saying 'Think carefully, My Lord, because the offering you accept will be the one you will receive henceforth, forever.'

"Zeus laughed and said, 'Then, my friend, Prometheus, you have made my choice even easier. I choose that offering,' and he pointed to the larger pile."

"So be it, I said," Prometheus gleefully interrupted Meliton. "And I strode over to the larger pile and grabbing the edge of the fat I pulled it aside to reveal that the fat was nothing more than the inner of the hide and when it fell away it exposed a pile of bones and offal."

He looked jubilantly at the two shepherds. "Zeus was astonished. 'Where's all the flesh and the heart?' he demanded, anger starting to redden his face. I walked over to the smaller pile and slit the stomach lining with a knife. All the best cuts of meat tumbled from it. The priests clapped, roared and laughed with delight."

"It is said that Zeus was angry at being tricked, thus," Meliton ventured.

"Angry?" Prometheus laughed, "He was beside himself. He hurled bolts of lightning about in a fury, causing considerable damage to the city and killing those priests who had laughed the loudest. I was lucky that he did not bind me to this rock then, but he decided to take it out on you mortals instead. His punishment was to take fire from you and hide it.

"That night I wandered amongst you mortals and saw the consequences of Zeus' action. People were tearing at hunks of raw meat and eating hard, uncooked vegetables, but the main problem was the cold. It was winter and a cold wind was whistling down Mount Olympus. People were dying of cold. Guilt drove her stake through my heart. This was my fault. Because I had made a fool of Zeus, you mortals were suffering and dying. I had seen where Zeus had hidden the fire, so I decided to sneak into his chambers and steal it back for humanity. I took the flower-head of a giant fennel plant with me and placed the flames amongst the yellow blossoms. It was easy. Zeus was still consumed by anger at being tricked and was stomping about his palace in a fury, not taking any notice of what was going on around him. I returned the fire to the mortals, but Zeus, of course, found out that it was I who had returned it. He was incandescent, and so here I am, chained to this rock for eternity," Prometheus finished resignedly. He looked up at the sky. "You must go," he ordered, suddenly. "Now! Go!"

His voice carried so much authority that we had no choice. We scuttled, like startled deer, back around the outcrop of rock, without a second glance back. Brutus was hot on our heels. But once behind the shelter of the rock, I paused. Something was wrong. Why was he suddenly so adamant that we leave? Something was about to happen – something that was probably outside the imagination of any mortal. I had to see what it was.

"I'm going back," I told Meliton. And, give him his due, although fear showed in his eyes, he did not hesitate to turn back with me. We stole back up the mountain track and, hiding behind the outcrop, we watched. My heart was beating as it had never done before.

*

I heard the chains rattle as they slithered across the altar stone. It was as if some invisible spirits were drawing them tight. Prometheus was hauled over the altar by the insistent tug of the chains. He did not appear to resist, but simply allowed himself to be positioned across the altar as if in resignation of his fate. When the chains stopped their rattling, Prometheus was stretched, spread-eagle across the smooth surface of the stone. A troubled silence fell over the mountain, even the cold wind died down. Everything seemed to be waiting in mute expectation. I could feel the cold, silent, leaden clouds weighing down on the world as though squeezing life from the very air itself. Then I vaguely became aware of a shift in the atmosphere, as though some monstrous presence was approaching. I scanned the skies, but all I saw was an eagle soaring in the grey heavens. As there was nothing else to attract my attention I watched as it soared majestically across the leaden skies. It soon became apparent that it was flying in our direction.

As it drew nearer I was struck with awe – it was immense. Were it not for the golden feathers I would have mistaken it for a dragon. It landed lightly beside the prone Prometheus, standing some six feet tall. My sense of awe turned to exaltation. Prometheus was saved. One of the gods must have sent this immense bird to tear up the chains and release the Titan. The eagle placed one of its huge, clawed feet on Prometheus' legs and its monstrous talons curled around his thighs and then, to my horror, it dropped its yellow beak and tore at Prometheus' abdomen. A scream of agony rent the air. It was the most horrific sound I had ever heard in my life. In a fury, I leapt forward from behind the rock and ran at the eagle, my staff raised, ready to…"

"You thought you could defeat a six-foot tall eagle with a shepherd's staff?" Isokrates asked, his voice dripping with incredulity.

Kleitos looked at the man. "It was all I had to hand."

"You could have run away."

"I wish he had," Meliton interjected.

"The thought did not cross my mind," Kleitos said in a matter-of-fact tone. "Here was someone who had fought for humanity and, as a result, he found himself chained to a rock and being consumed by an eagle of godly proportions. I just thought I needed to go to his aid."

"And you survived?" asked Isokrates, doubtfully.

"Not quite, but I shall leave that part of the tale to Meliton, as my recollection of what happened next is somewhat vague." He looked at his fellow shepherd.

*

I nearly evacuated my bowels when I saw my master rushing towards the beast. But I had no choice but to follow. Loading my sling, I dashed after him. Brutus was at his master's heels, barking furiously.

The noise drew the eagle's attention and with a shrill, spine-chilling keen of anger and a single massive beat of its wings, it lifted itself over the altar and landed in front of my master.

Behind the bird I had the vague sense of Prometheus shouting furiously for us to get away and not to interfere.

The bird lowered its vicious beak at my master and he struck it with a well-aimed blow to the head. The bird reared up in anger and thrust a clawed foot at him. My master beat at its reptilian leg as the talons curled around his body. My stones flew at its head, but seemed to have no more effect than a snowflake landing on the back of an ox. The bird lowered its gaping maw at my master. It seemed nothing could stop it from ripping my master asunder, but Brutus sunk his teeth into the back of the bird's massive, yellow leg. The bird shrilled in pain and turned on the dog, releasing my master.

He lay there, lifeless. I rushed forward and, grasping his wrists, pulled his bloody body down the track to safety beyond the rocky outcrop. I dashed back to call Brutus off the bird, but I was too late. The brave animal lay ripped apart on the cold rocky ground. The eagle had turned back to Prometheus and I, in a fury over the killing of Brutus, hurled stone after stone at it. But it took no notice of my attack as it ripped the guts from Prometheus and devoured his liver. Then with a scream of victory it lifted itself from the altar stone, the beat of its wings almost knocking me from my feet. I stood, breathless and awestruck, watching the gigantic bird fly back from where it had come. A groan from the altar drew me from my reverie. I walked cautiously over to the altar stone.

Prometheus lay there, his abdomen was torn open. Blood flowed from the horrific wound, but he turned his head to me as I approached. Even in the increasing gloom, I could see the agony etched on his features.

"You're alive?" I gasped, unable to tear my eyes from the gaping, bloody mess that was all that was left of his stomach.

"I'm immortal," he said acerbically. "Where is that foolish friend of yours?"

"I dragged him to safety."

"Is he alive?"

"I don't know."

"Go and check. If he's still alive, bring him to me."

I turned and scrambled across the rough ground and around the outcrop. I dropped to my knees beside my master. His clothes were in ruins and blood seeped from deep gashes where the eagle's talons had sliced his flesh. I lowered my ear to his mouth. His breath was so shallow it was difficult to hear, but he was breathing. I cradled him and lifted him. He moaned. I carried him back to the altar stone. I noted the chains had loosened and Prometheus was able to move his limbs freely. He shifted cautiously to one side of the altar top.

"Place him beside me."

I did as I was commanded and Prometheus rested an arm across my master's body.

"Has the food arrived?"

I looked into the deepening shadows at the base of the rock.

"It has," I nodded.

"Then eat what you need and sleep."

I crouched down beside the cold altar and tried to eat some food and drink a little wine but found I had no appetite. I curled into a tight ball, against the increasing cold and watched the grey skies darken to night. I fell into a fitful sleep, which was interrupted by nightmarish images and the bitter cold. Eventually, I crawled across the icy rocks and collected the body of Brutus. I dragged it back to the shelter of the altar and hugged the animal to me like a blanket. It was the longest night of my life, but I dared not look at the top of the altar – some sense told me to do so would send me out of my mind.

I did fall asleep and when I stirred the next morning, stiff from the cold and the hardness of my bed, I became aware of someone sitting beside me. I started awake. It was Prometheus.

"Did you sleep well?" he asked.

I did not answer. Instead my eyes ran rudely over his body as he sat there casually eating breakfast. There was not a mark on his body.

"Did I dream it? Did I dream about the eagle and …," my voice came to a croaking halt.

"No."

"Then how are you alive, and sitting beside me? There is no wound. It is as if it never happened."

"Oh, it happened alright and will again this evening and again tomorrow and for the rest of my immortal life."

I stared at him in horror. "But how…?"

He looked at me ruefully, as a man resigned to his fate. "That is the brilliance of Zeus' punishment. I am immortal. Each evening the eagle comes and rips me open and devours my liver. The following night I heal, only to have the eagle visit the following day and repeat the process."

"That's grotesque!"

Prometheus laughed. "It's genius."

"My Master! He's not immortal!" I stood up and looked onto the altar top. My master lay there. The wounds had healed to ugly scars and he was as still as a corpse. "Is he... dead?"

"No, he's sleeping. He's been through quite an ordeal. As have you. I thank you for your bravery, even though it was misplaced. There is nothing you could do to help. This is my fate, from now until eternity."

I was not really listening, for my master had stirred. I leant over him and called his name. His eyes flashed open. He sat up quickly, but moaned in discomfort.

"Ah, Master Kleitos, you have woken," Prometheus observed.

My master looked around anxiously.

"The eagle has gone," I assured him.

"I'm starving," he announced.

"Come, join me for some breakfast," said Prometheus.

My master heaved himself from the altar and sat down beside the Titan. They ate heartily and in comradely silence.

"So, My Lord," my master broke the silence, "there is nothing we can do to help you?"

"No," Prometheus responded shortly. "But I thank you for trying."

My master laughed. "It was a rather pathetic attempt."

"But brave beyond any measure. Here, let me see your

wounds."

My master removed the tattered remnants of his clothes and Prometheus examined him. He frowned. "That is the best I could do," he said. "I am sorry about the scars that you will be left with."

My master smiled. "I shall bear them with honour, My Lord."

"Good. I have a gift for you, for both of you. I cannot make you immortal. But I would not wish that on anyone, anyway. However, I will gift you both a very long and very healthy life. Now go, my friends. I do not want to become too attached to you, because it will make my loneliness all the worse once you have gone."

We stood up and bowed to the god. As we turned to go a thought came to me.

"My Lord?"

He looked up at me, a smile cut across his face. "Hercules," he said, before I could ask my question. "The only one who may be able to break my chains is Hercules."

I bowed at him once more. "Then, My Lord, I shall find him and bring him to you."

"I would appreciate that very much," he grinned at me.

We turned and left.

*

Their audience stared at them in stunned silence.

Then Isokrates guffawed loudly. The moment was broken

and the men around the table burst into laughter. Isokrates slapped the table gleefully.

"That is the best tale I have heard in my life, Kleitos." He turned and shouted across the room, "Barman, bring Kleitos and Meliton a tumbler of your very best mead." He looked back at the old shepherd. "Kleitos, I never knew you could tell such tales. You had me on the edge of my seat." He laughed merrily, running his eyes joyfully around the table of chuckling men. The serious look he got when his gaze returned to Kleitos caused his merriment to falter. He looked from Kleitos to Meliton. Their grave expressions did not alter.

"Come, Kleitos, you're not going to tell me that your story is true... are you?"

"I am."

Kleitos started to rise slowly. Meliton assisted him up.

"Remove my shirt," he said to Meliton.

Meliton lifted the old, worn shirt above the old man's head. The others all leaned forward. Gasps rose from their lips as they saw the ragged lines of red scars running around his torso. Isokrates ran a finger along one of the welts.

"By all the gods," he whispered hoarsely. "It's true." He looked the old man in the eye. "Why have you never told us about this before?"

The old man shrugged as he put his shirt back on. "I suppose, because I am not a boastful man," he said with a glint in his eye.

His friends burst out laughing and slapped Isokrates on the back. He grinned sheepishly. Then a thought struck him. He held his hand up for silence and looked Meliton in the eye.

"So, did you seek and find Hercules, as you promised?"

Meliton went to speak, but Kleitos placed a hand gently on his arm.

"That, my friend" Kleitos said, wryly, giving Isokrates a wink, "is another story, for another time."

[This short story has been published separately as *Prometheus*]

La Accabadora e Las Roccas

Steven Battersby

It's well past the end of summer, although, high on this rugged Galluran hillside, it's still hot by my standards. I am sweating and out of breath. My eyes are smarting with saltiness. My right wrist is in agony. And most of all, I am deeply unhappy. Despite the beautiful rocky surroundings I regret being here. Even the distant tinkling of sheep bells in the brightly shimmering air and the sweet scent of the glorious pink and white oleanders everywhere, so unusual to me and so enticing when I first arrived here, now fail to attract me. Bright green lizards scuttling, almost too late, across the stony path away from my trudging feet, no longer entertain me. Why did I ever come here? I am "tutto rimpianto" (all regret) and I just wish I could start again and that things would work out differently.

Not watching where I'm going, I stray from the narrow track and around some horse-sized boulders. They are angular and wind-sculpted, balancing in their own shadows on strangely fin-shaped granite legs. Now that I'm away from the path, I think I will be alone with my thoughts. But instead here are these crazy ancient animal-like rocks and suddenly, as it seems, they surround me like a silent and hungry pack. I look about me and try to swallow while they crouch amongst the dry shrubs and watch unwelcomingly.

"You're not one of us. That makes you guilty," they seem to be judging me. I self-consciously try to find the fastest way back to the track away from them. I feel vulnerable and entirely out of place in their presence. Then I am caught in a patch of large thistles and step backwards to escape their spiky grip. A Sardinian Swallowtail butterfly floats elegantly away from me upwards into the cloudless sky but, although my gaze follows as it fades into the blue distance, I am disinterested. In sight of the path now, I stop walking and my head hangs in lonely sorrow as I try to piece together what has happened today. I hold my crumpled straw hat to stop it falling off my head. The sun is bright enough to burn my scalp, though Sardinians would explain that this weather is what they call "fresco" and they dress warmly anyway.

Why did I ever come here? The short answer is easy – I have always believed myself to be a curious person, and I've wanted to satisfy my curiosity about Sardinia. But at the same time, I now realise I've simply been too arrogant to notice what is really going on. There are so many other questions I should have asked, but now it is too late. Here am I in my early seventies and I've only just started to understand about so much of the real world, the world that really matters, which I've never even thought to notice!

Of course, it's more complicated than that. Let me explain. I'm Bill Nelis, the well-published Oxford archaeologist. Have you read any of the beautifully illustrated books by Dr Nelis? No? Well, never mind. I am told they were popular in Italy back in the 1970's. I've recently been working in Sardinia with two colleagues, one amateur and one professional, on the excavation of a small site. The site, of course, is unimportant by itself; it's just a heap of rubble from the remains of a small nuraghe, and maybe it pre-dates the bronze age... But no, no, no! This level of detail is not clarifying anything. Although I do still feel inside that I am an archaeologist – how could I ever not – my working life has now, this day, ended. What can I, professionally-speaking, honestly give to the world now that I appreciate my own blindness to what's around me? I simply don't know what I have to offer now. But how have I so suddenly reached this point? Let me explain.

Our dig is presently unattended and I suppose the work there will now never be finished. A big cause for regret. Well... we had such a small grant for the work, you see – that's how it always is in Sardinia – never quite enough money for anything of antiquity to be studied properly. But don't worry about the nuraghe, that's just the official reason for my coming here. I really came over here to discreetly test a new scanning and survey technique of my own devising, to do "Geophys" in a place where nobody would ask or notice, where I could try out my equipment, and nobody would talk. Sardinia would surely be a good place to keep my work secret until it was ready to be presented to a grateful world.

"What's a nuraghe?" you ask. So, nuraghes are one of the great Neolithic mysteries of Sardinia, amongst all of its other Neolithic – and older – mysteries, of course. A nuraghe is a stone tower, built with really enormous rocks, and I mean really enormous, but carefully worked by ancient stone hands using basic stone tools into the perfect shape for building. Let's just say that the men in Nuraghic times must have been very strong. Small, but very strong indeed. How were these towers constructed to be so tall? Who made them? Why did they make them? Were they religious sites or defensive prehistoric castles? Or both? These are all questions without answers, except we do know that there are thousands and thousands of them all over the island. Many of them – probably most of them for all I know – have become buried in natural hills of their own making over the course of thousands of years, so that even the Romans, mining them two thousand years later for the shaped stone that they contained, only found the top layers, leaving it to modern archaeology to discover the structures now hidden below ground.

But listen, it's not the nuraghe or the archaeology or even my ground-scanning equipment (which worked, by the way – I always knew it would!), none of that matters now. None of that would have ever made me really open my eyes. No, it's the people, or rather one person in particular, that I want to talk about, so let me introduce them.

Our team is – was – small, being just the three of us.

Obviously myself, Bill, as Director of Archaeology. Then there was Claudio as our labourer – though, of course, he was much more than just that. His father, Signor Vanni, owns all the land around (and is a great winemaker too), so for work in the school holidays he has sent his youngest son to keep an eye on what we've been doing.

On our first day Signor Vanni said in no uncertain terms, although he laughed as he said it, "You can dig here, and only here, but you touch the soil near my vines or you touch my grapes at all and it will be curtains for you!" Claudio brought us wine and bread from his generous father every day after that for our lunch. What a great lad Claudio is, and a hard worker, too, for the small amount of money he's earned. We left all the physical work to him, we really did, but we let him do none of the delicate archaeology.

And there's Nizia. Lovely, trustworthy Fenizia Tanit, surely so full of energy and vitality. Well that's how I saw it. My feisty thirty-something assistant archaeo in T-shirt and jeans, with a long black plait and those dark heavily made-up brown eyes and sun-tanned arms. Actually, I didn't know her age at all – didn't think to ask – and just guessed at early thirties. Nizia, who spoke English so fluently and bluntly and, like so many Sardinians, had trained and worked somewhere abroad but now returned because she couldn't bear to be away from the island any longer. Ha! But she really did call a spade a spade! And most of it was directed vigorously at Claudio who just couldn't understand why we were excavating sometimes with paintbrushes when a pickaxe would be so much faster. She liked her T-shirts to have short English messages, usually rude. I remember her favourite one that shouted "What do you want NOW!" in huge letters on the front... oh dear, actually she was wearing that the last time I saw her at the dig.

Although Claudio and I both walked across the hills to the site in the morning, Nizia always drove in her dented, rusting old Mini, which would never have passed its MOT in England.

She came from a village in a nearby valley, too far, she said, for pedalling a bike. Really, it was near enough and would have been an easy ride, but I never asked why she preferred to drive. Although she always arrived promptly in the morning and was sometimes at work even before me, her routine was to leave earlier than us. As she explained, "Someone has to put Mamma to bed". We could often hear her shouting at somebody on her mobile through the open window as her car bumped its uneasy way across the rough ground back towards the road. Those times, Claudio and I used to look at each other and laugh once she'd gone, and then he enjoyed copying her, pretending to shout "ciao, ciao, ciao, ciao, ciao!" into an invisible mobile phone clamped between shoulder and cheek whilst steering, smoking and changing gear all at the same time.

This situation with the three of us was all fine and suited me perfectly. That was the time towards the end of the day when I could scan the ground beyond our official site, using my prototype geophysics kit, while I left Claudio doing some sieving. There is a small hillock near us, but right above the vineyard – I am convinced now that there is something of real significance beneath the ground there. Something more than a nuraghe. Something much older and deeper. I told Claudio I was just electronically testing the pH of the soil if anyone were to ask. Actually, I was gradually building up a 3d scan of the layers beneath, down to about ten metres – but sorry – the details will never matter now, will they?

I'd kept all this to myself and, now that I trusted her, I finally wanted to tell Nizia, but away from Claudio overhearing. His father would be very, let's say, "unforgiving" if he found out I had trespassed. So I had spoken to her quietly, like a conspirator, as we crouched down in the sunshine to inspect some Mycenaean pottery shards in situ, our heads bent close together. Somehow I'd never spoken to her about anything so personal, and this moment felt awkward.

"Nizia, there's something I want to say to you, Something I've been meaning to tell you for some time. It can't wait. Meet me tonight…" I had begun, surprised at the nervous quaver in my own voice, and then tailed off as she had stood up away from me, holding up her hand signalling me to stop right there, where I still crouched.

"You and me on a date? Really Dr Nelis?" She took half a threatening step towards me, put on a loud mock-Italian accent whilst pointing down at me and then back at herself in pantomime fashion: "Older English man thinks naive Sardinian country-girl is push-over!" she said this with an enormous comic frown, then laughed as she watched me blush with uncomfortable indignation. My mouth dropped open as I then realised it was her kind of a joke, and she continued "Don't worry Bill, I know you don't mean anything like that. At least you had better not. We know each other too well for that, don't we? Well what is it?"

I was still embarrassed because I'd not realised my own fondness for her, until she had put it so succinctly. "Typical," I muttered in English, trying to recover as my blush cooled, countering with an open-handed gesture, "Always right about everything, as usual." And then, pointing at myself, with the same mock-Italian accent "Men! Always so predictable!" I stopped smiling. I realised that perhaps I didn't know her as well as I thought. "Seriously, Nizia. Please. It's something I can't say in front of Claudio. It's something his father can't find out right now," I started to explain. But Claudio had reappeared pushing the wheel-barrow and I'd had to clam up.

Later, she had quietly agreed, while she rested in the shade during one of our breaks, to meet me for dinner at the Hotel Svegliati once her mother's housework was done.

But she made it clear she still wanted an early night herself, though she didn't say why.

At the end of the day Claudio set off through the vineyards, swinging his lanky way casually downhill to his home, and I walked around the slope in the other direction back to my B&B in San Pasquale. As usual, I puzzled over the granite formations that I could see at the top of the next hillside. Geologists always supposed them to be entirely natural formations. These wind-sculpted Galluran white granite rocks, in many shapes and sizes, but of a type which could be seen dotted all over the landscape around here, were something quite special. The imagination turned many into fantastical creatures. But I was not so sure that at least some hadn't had considerable human help with their appearance in some very ancient, prehistoric time. Of course, by now, there would probably be no surviving evidence for this, but it would be worth checking one day if I had time.

In the far distance, for example, I could see what looked very plainly to be a giant stone bear looking out to sea. On a hill nearer to me was what looked like a pair of enormous stone turtles, posed as though facing each other. I guessed that the height of the larger was some fifty feet, and the smaller a good twenty feet. They stood on sturdy legs, and I felt that the front legs of the larger one really did resemble powerful flippers. This one was reared right up as if about to attack the smaller one. Well, however you looked, there was something rather chilling and disturbing about the whole scene in the gathering gloom, natural rock formation or not. There was no doubt that both had the beaks of turtles, but of course if they'd ever had anything that chanced to look like eyes, those would have been eroded completely away over the millennia.

Both turtles were really part of a larger formation of heavily eroded caves, spreading further round the hill, which at some point in the past had been turned into stables, now disused. You could see its dilapidated drystone walling from here. I recall that evening that I had resolved to go over and have a better look in full daylight before I left for England. But, of course, as I walked happily down to the village, I had no premonition of what was to come.

There had been no need to book a table at the Svegliati. With the holiday season over, the village was now all but deserted. I'd sat down at seven, as we'd agreed, and the waitress had laid the table for two in unsmiling silence, her only words being in English "Bread? Water jug?" And so I had sat and waited by myself for almost two hours before finally grumpily ordering a plate of horse steak and fried potatoes, then finding my way home for the night, rather disappointed. I remember very clearly on the walk back, wondering if perhaps Nizia hadn't turned up because she really thought I was trying it on with her; and then realising that I didn't even know if she was in a relationship anyway. But surely she had joked about our "date", hadn't she, so perhaps her getting her mother to bed had been too much trouble, or something else important had come up. I hoped there would be a sensible reason, and anyway there would be other evenings or opportunities to discuss my discovery in this last week before I had to return to Oxford. I had hesitated and hesitated about phoning her until it had become too late to disturb her – something else I will regret to my dying day.

In the morning, I thought perhaps I would arrive at work early as no doubt she would too. Then we could speak quickly before Claudio arrived.

So the next day, getting up while it was still dark, I skipped breakfast, chose some jam tarts and a chunk of pecorino cheese from the kitchen to have later, and set off in the cool shadows just before the dawn. I walked easily on the path across the macchia hillside beyond the village, knapsack on one shoulder, carrying my straw hat in one hand and holding an unlit cigarette in the other. When I worked abroad, I thoroughly enjoyed playing the part of the stylish English archaeologist, though at home I never smoked and certainly would never be seen wearing a straw hat.

I glanced over at the pair of rock turtles as I went past. The locals simply called them Las Roccas. Really, in the shadows, the larger one did look enormous and menacing, maybe even with its beak open; the smaller one really did look as if it was cowering. I glanced at my watch and decided to spend maybe five minutes having a closer look to see if there were any signs of hammer marks or tell-tale ancient percussion flakes on the underside of the turtle shells.

Breaking away from the path, I moved across the shallow valley and up the hillside towards Las Roccas, skirting around a large patch of prickly pears. I was sure I saw the silhouette of a woman dressed entirely in black moving away from me, just beyond the rocks. I was certain I had. It was hard to see, I was maybe still five hundred yards away, but I was convinced she turned and glanced at me and quickened her pace once she saw me. She was holding something narrow and black – or perhaps just a small bundle of black cloth – tucked tightly under one arm. Intrigued, I too quickened my pace up the hill, jumping over rocks, pushing through thorny bushes and breaking off flower buds from others in my haste. Within a few minutes I was standing right where I had last seen her. I looked all around, but she had disappeared. As I say, it was hard to see in the blueish-purple light just before dawn, but I was sure she was wearing what looked like a long black gown right down to her feet, with a black hood. When she had looked at me, it seemed her face was wrinkled and outlined with grey hair, and I imagined that if she was an old widow, then perhaps she could only walk slowly.

On realising that she had vanished so suddenly, I was pierced by an instant of irrational fear and I shivered. Then

I thought again about my work and the moment of cold dread passed. I had promised myself just five minutes to look at the rocks and so I moved over purposely towards the granite turtles.

Right beneath the head of the smaller one appeared to be someone sleeping on the ground. I tip-toed cautiously forward to take a look. Just then I glanced up at the motionless stone creatures above the sleeping figure. The rising sun had lit up the silent, open beak of the larger one, a vivid crimson, whilst all else remained in shadow. The sight of its mute cry to the empty sky, frozen in red, is a sight I will never forget.

I crept closer, not wanting to seem nosy, yet overwhelmed by curiosity. As the light improved, I realised that it was Nizia that I was seeing, laying motionless on the ground. She was on her back, her uncovered legs straight out and her arms by her sides, not in the usual rude T-shirt and jeans, but in a simple armless short white dress. Maybe it was a nightie. Her voluminous black hair, now unplaited, was even longer, and was laid over her chest from both sides of her head, reaching almost to her waist. The low neckline of her dress revealed some indistinct green and black tattoo in her cleavage. Usually this part of her body was covered by her high-necked T-shirt – the tattoo revealing something about her I had never known, a private clue to a previous life abroad that she had not shared with me, and about which I had never thought to ask.

I was mortally embarrassed to be looking at her like this. It was such a strange and haunting scene. I made a noise to wake her, kicking my foot through some stones accidentally on purpose, whilst quickly trying to work out some words to explain my spying on her. Although... how was I to know she would have spent the night outside wearing next to nothing?

She did not wake, and so I loudly called her name, "Nizia, Nizia! What are you doing here? You must be cold outside at this time of day. Put this on," I took off my knapsack and moved closer, proffering my tweed waistcoat, expecting her to sit up at any moment.

The pounding in my chest became unbearable as I looked ever more closely. My legs suddenly became weak. A trail of ants struggled in the blood that shone dark red on the white gravel under her head. I quickly knelt and squeezed her hand laid at the side of her body. Her fingers were cold and unresponsive. I dropped the dead hand and recoiled in shock and panic, falling clumsily backwards over my knapsack as I struggled to stand up. I tried to breathe normally and felt intense pain in my right wrist where I had fallen. My mobile was in my knapsack. I fumbled uselessly with my left hand to get it out and dialled 118 for an ambulance.

*

As her body was being carried away on a stretcher to the

ambulance parked at the bottom of the hill, a Carabinieri Officer helped me to my feet and handed my waistcoat and crumpled hat back to me. He gently questioned me, repeating himself whenever I couldn't understand his Sassari Sardinian accent. I told him everything that had happened, everything I knew, everything just as I have told you. Claudio was somehow there too. Now I could see he had been crying. He was young; I imagined he had never seen death before. It was fully daylight and the sky was bright and the air was so clear. I remember seeing crickets hopping across the gravel, flashing red or sometimes green as they leapt. I remember everything in vivid detail about that morning.

I explained my surprise at seeing her outside when surely she must have stayed in to put her mother early to bed, and Claudio shook his head and smiled sadly as the Officer continued to take notes. I found I couldn't say her name, couldn't say it. So I just said "Si" whenever the Officer wanted to clarify that I meant Signorina Tanit. This was when I noticed that my wrist must have been bandaged earlier by the ambulance-men.

Claudio spoke up in clear Italian. "Signor Nelis, you have misunderstood about the Signorina. Her mother died a year ago and her father many years before that. She was never putting her mother to bed early when she finished work, but herself, did you not know? Her father used to work at the winery with my father. Her family are old friends of ours, she was… she was Aunt Fenizia to me when I was little. I will miss her dreadfully." He broke off and looked away with his hands covering the shame of his wet cheeks, as we heard the ambulance pulling away.

We paused until there was silence once more. "Claudio, I'm sorry. You never let on that you knew her, except from work. She shouted and swore at you so much. You made so much fun of her behind her back. How would I have ever guessed?"

"Si Signor, my Aunt certainly made me laugh. And you. But Signor, you never asked. So I thought you knew. Everyone knows everyone around here. We all do," Claudio smiled seriously as he swung his arm in a wide arc across the landscape. The Officer nodded knowingly in agreement and put his notebook smartly away. It was clear that somehow my interview was over.

"Officer, what has happened? Please - is this murder or an accident? There is another witness. The old widow I saw – she saw all this before I did. We must find her and ask her… and also what was she carrying away…" but the Officer cut me short with a single word of explanation.

"Accabadora."

I didn't understand. How could I?

"Signor, you will not find La Accabadora," continued Claudio, "my Aunt Fenizia had a disease. We all knew. I do not know it in English. It is called MNM - Malattia del Neurone di Motore. We are all ready for this day. She always wanted to stay young, but now she has reached forty-five years old. Yes signor, she is more than forty – really old, eh?" he repeated on seeing my obvious surprise.

"Sometimes she had bad days, bad-bad days, when she was in America, when it was cold even in the Summer. So she came back home to Gallura where it is only cold for a short time in Winter. She feared the Winter and now it is the end of the Summer, so she was afraid. The disease only gets worse, never better. Every Winter more to fear than the last."

He stopped speaking as if this was an explanation that would help me.

I noticed the Carabinieri Officer had found her mobile nearby and was pushing buttons as he checked the numbers dialled. He put the phone in his pocket, nodding gravely and then he looked me straight in the eye.

"Si. La Femina Accabadora. There will be no investigation, Signor. No-one here would wish it. We do not investigate this type of death. This was not murder, but it was also not an accident. Do you understand? She died quickly without pain. A sharp colpire to the back of the head. Everything is in order. This is what is required of the Accabadora and no more. She only comes to do her work when she is called and when she is sure she is needed."

The Officer gripped my sagging shoulder while the realisation sank in about what had happened. I remembered hearing from somewhere a version of the old Sardinian myth of the woman from a long-distant past dressed sombrely in black who only came at night. It was just a scary legend, it was never true. Who made up these strange old folk tales? In the story she was some old witch who came secretly at night with her cudgel only out of extreme necessity to help some poor soul humanely pass on when they were painfully outliving their natural time or were now suffering incurable illness in their old age.

"I… I need some time by myself, sorry, sorry, I'm so sorry," I stammered in bad Italian, and turned away to look at the far-reaching view towards the sea across the rugged countryside. The flowers on the oleander bushes nearby had opened, pink on some and white on others. The scent was, I suppose, beautiful, but in my state with welling eyes and a hard lump in my throat I could smell nothing. I trudged slowly away.

The Wrath of Grapes
David Lloyd

Peter Stone was in a quandary. Across from him sat three perfect bottles of wine with a value in excess of £15,000. The only drawback was that they did not belong to him.

He had devoted his life to learning about wine – initially helping out as a seasonal worker at numerous vineyards abroad and then training to be a sommelier in the UK, his place of origin. He sat numerous wine education qualifications and worked hard to network with growers, retail suppliers and restaurants. By the time he reached 50, he owned a stake in a small vineyard in Ontario, Canada, and had a reputation for helping others up the ladder to success. He knew he would never be one of the world's greats, but he had made a good career out of something he loved.

He lived in quintessential England, enjoying the serenity of the Cotswolds, so – for many folk he had achieved an idyllic life, spending much of it wine tasting, hosting events and visiting new vineyards emerging in Europe.

His real passion was entertaining – speaking at events and amusing people with his wit and remarkable tales of wine while educating people in tasting and pairing. Perhaps it was the emphasis on pairing in the last five years that had taken its toll on his body? He was two stone heavier than five years previously – and he didn't want to think about the total increase in his weight since a decade ago.

Large and jolly? Yes, he fitted that caricature, but there was a hidden sadness that he deliberately kept secret – a diagnosis, an aneurism that could strike at any moment. Now celebrating his sixtieth birthday, he knew this milestone would be his last – and celebrating it wasn't so easy. His long-time partner had traded him for a younger model two years ago, and he had no children to show for the 30-year marriage.

Thus, Pete had come to be alone on this so-called special day, but at least he was enjoying one of the most interesting tasks of his career to date. Every now and then, he would be recommended among the wealthy echelons of society as someone who is trustworthy and able to accurately value wines in any cellar in preparation for sale or auction. On this occasion, the death of 85-year-old widower and entrepreneur Barry Abrams had led to his two spoilt sons eagerly wanting to sell off the family mansion and all its contents 'at the earliest opportunity'. The contents included a purpose-built temperature-controlled wine cellar with more than a thousand bottles of wines from across Europe, the New World and North America. And while Pete began this task, other specialists moved around the house, too – art valuers, antique dealers and classic car experts.

But Pete's job was by far the most arduous. Initially he

said the task would take two weeks but then the heirs had said he could stay in the home if he would finish the task in one. Pete jumped at the opportunity and thus became resident in the mansion, accompanied only by a rather surly housekeeper, Mrs Jones, and a part-time cook – both of whom were working their notice.

Remarkably, there was nothing in the way of an inventory – most extraordinary given the amazing care that had obviously been taken in the construction of the cellar and building up the wine collection. No doubt some notes and records were buried somewhere, but the family had scoured the entire house and their father's computer before finally asking Pete to record every wine and build up the inventory from scratch. This was a much tougher task, since he would also need to compile notes on each for the impending auction – but for that he had additional time since the auction would be three months' away.

As Pete moved between the well-organised racks in the first couple of days, a wry smile would occasionally flicker across his face, only for the next wines to invoke a perplexed and bemused look. Pete had already concluded that the owner was a gambler with wine: his eclectic and extravagant selections were fascinating, but very much hit and miss.

After the racks of visible bottles, all lying on their sides, he turned his attention to the cases, all stacked carefully but in various corners of the cellar. And then, at precisely

4.10pm on day three, Pete's face lit up in a way that it had never done before.

He was busy recording what looked like another sealed case of twelve Chateau Pontet-Canet, a delicious Pauillac from 2007, but, in the interest of thoroughness, he double-checked and found the case to be open after removing an old cloth partially covering the top. Rather than twelve bottles, there were just three resting peacefully together, side-by-side on a bed of straw, with each one immediately being visibly different from the other.

Pete's heart would always race quickly when he beheld the necks of unknown bottles, just like a child who feels he is about to discover buried treasure in a hidden chest.

Intrigued, Pete lifted them out carefully, one-by-one, placing them on the table in front of him, ensuring the labels were turned away from him. In that way, he would turn one at a time and learn about each one, keeping the excitement alive for as long as possible. Somehow he already knew that three of the most remarkable wines he had ever laid eyes on were in front of him, their identities just a 180 degree turn.

The first he turned was the white wine – a 1971 Joh. Jos. Prum Wehlener Sonnenuhr Riesling Trockenbeerenauslese from a vineyard that had been in the same family since the 17th century. Pete might have missed its importance had he not given a talk recently on sweet wines and quipped about the range of prices – this one valued at probably more than £3,000. He had tasted sweet wines at £300 a bottle, but this one was in a completely different league.

He paused to admire it, and googled it to be sure he wasn't over-estimating it or overlooking anything. But he wasn't, and he sat in awe of it, believing that he had looked at the best one first.

But wine number two was not in any way inferior - a 1999 Henri Jayer Cros Parantoux, Vosne-Romanée Premier Cru from France. Pete knew all about this full-bodied Burgundy and had once visited the small vineyard. His head imagined a £5,000 price tag but he would need to look into this in more depth when his excitement died down. All he could do now was marvel at such a find. Never had he anticipated such pleasure, least of all on his birthday.

He leaned over and turned bottle number three expecting to be disappointed, but a 1975 Domaine de la Romanée-Conti Grand Cru, Cote de Nuits could never disappoint. At least 85% Pinot noir grape, he found himself gazing intensely at the perfect Burgundy. He googled it and smiled as he read that the Archbishop of Paris once described it as 'velvet and satin in bottles'. This one may be double the cost of the previous bottle, Pete thought to himself.

For more than an hour, Pete just stared at the bottles, reading the labels, checking the authenticity of each and the seal of the corks. They were in perfect condition, and Pete didn't know whether to laugh or cry for joy. He did both. And he embraced each bottle in turn as if the proud father of triplets.

It was at this time that he realised two dominant thoughts were vying for his attention. Firstly, on occasions of finding such remarkable treasure or indeed much lesser treasure, he always celebrated with a glass or three of wine. And fortunately the sons had told him that he could drink the wine stored in the kitchen, should he wish to imbibe, so he was naturally contemplating this.

But thought number two was a much more challenging one. He was sitting in a cellar of a thousand or so wines for which there was no inventory, including the three in front of him, each calling out to be lovingly admired and, yes, tasted.

Pete broke out into a sudden sweat, cursing himself for even thinking such a thought. In his 38 years in the trade, he had never done such a thing. But the idea would not go away.

He thought of the two rightful owners, the errant sons who were both set to become multi-millionaires thanks to their father's remarkable art collection and range of antiques. The sons knew nothing of the wine, nor did they particularly care for it. They both had a reputation for womanising, poor investments and betting on the horses – and no doubt the new funds would eventually be squandered in this way.

Then Pete thought of his own situation, the ticking time bomb of the aneurism, and how he would never get another chance to taste the wine of the gods.

Somehow the discussion in his head moved from the thought of 'Should I open one?' to 'Should I open one now?' The Henri Jayer, perhaps? And then he could save the other two, one for each day as he finished up the inventory? Or should he smuggle them all out so he could enjoy them in the comfort of his living room? And perhaps he could invite a friend or two to indulge with him - but he knew he could never trust anyone with such a secret or expect them to understand.

Then he smiled to himself as he explored various new ideas. What if he were to call together some of the top wine tasters and put these wines to them, pretending they were from his own vineyard in Canada? Or maybe he would throw a dinner party for friends and rebottle the wine so no one would know what amazing wines they were really tasting. Or maybe, he mused, just drink one bottle now and have the other two for a party. So many options.

He rose, more excited than he had ever known himself to be, returned the bottles gently into the case, and went back upstairs to see if all was clear so he could take the wine into the main house. Immediately he bumped into the cook who announced that dinner was ready, a rather early dinner because he had to visit his mother in hospital later.

"We're having beef, if you want to choose a wine?" he said, nodding over to the kitchen cellar. "I'll let you choose again since you're the expert."

"Delighted to do so. Oddly enough, I was just thinking about a glass of red. Hazard of my trade, I guess," quipped Pete.

The cook smiled, and added that Mrs Jones would be joining them. Pete selected a wine and began to regale his small audience of two over dinner with stories of the wine world. No one could have guessed the inner turmoil that Pete was feeling – nor the sense he had that this simple two-course meal seemed to last an interminable length of time. Was the devil himself goading him with temptation then denying the opportunity, removing the golden moment of pleasure? Was the velvet and satin that the Archbishop described more velvet and Satan?

At last, Pete was able to excuse himself at the end of the meal, saying he was behind on the inventory and wanted to put in another couple of hours. He grabbed two fresh wine glasses and the remainder of the bottle, and said he would finish it in the cellar. There were, of course, no objections.

Pete felt excitement race through his veins as he made his way back to the crate. He breathed a sigh of relief to see these beautiful bottles once again, to be able to cherish them and know that earlier was not a dream.

Again he stared at each bottle in turn, appreciating each for their different characters, histories and celebrity status. There was no turning back. With an otherwise unblemished career, surely Pete was allowed a little deviation without repercussion? Yes, he convinced himself, this was the case.

And it wasn't too difficult to do.

Without further ado, the 1999 Burgundy was uncorked. He sniffed the cork and smiled. He then poured the first glass but would now tease himself and not touch it for an hour, allowing it to breathe. In a moment of sheer hedonism, he reached for the second red, chuckling to himself as never before, as he uncorked it. He placed his nose to the neck of the bottle and breathed in deeply, as he had done with the first. The scents made him even giddier. He sniffed the corks again before placing them as souvenirs into his pocket. Yes, tonight was going to be a proper, albeit unexpected, 60th birthday celebration.

He poured a small glass of the 1975 Domaine de la Romanée-Conti into the second glass he had with him. Always take two wine glasses wherever you go, he thought to himself, because that way you never drink alone.

With both bottles breathing happily, Pete stood up, smiled at the wines and walked over to the stairs to check there would be no disturbances. In the kitchen, he found no one there – the cook and housekeeper had clearly finished for the evening, exactly as he had hoped.

The house had the most beautiful of libraries, more than a thousand books on dark oak shelves, with a range of chairs to suit every reader and every back disorder. The chaise longue, although decadent, might have been good for being fed grapes but it was not suitable for drinking wine. However, there was a lovely leather Chesterfield with a small round oak table next to it and Pete had this clearly in his mind. He could not dream of a more suitable room anywhere in the world than this treasure trove to celebrate his birthday.

He made his way there, along the corridor, passing the formal dining room and main lounge before entering his place of choice. He found the light switches, keeping them dim, while moving to the Chesterfield to turn on the reading lamp. Although the light outside was fading, the view out into the garden and over the fields was stunning, and Pete sensed a remarkable sunset in the making, with the skies beginning to turn red and pink. Yes, now was the time to go back and collect his new friends from the cellar.

He retraced his steps to the cellar, with every pace gaining in confidence that tonight was his night: everything was in place. He gathered his two full wine glasses, his phone and his notebook, and once again smiled at the wines before him. "I'll be back for you in a minute, my friends," he whispered.

Pete had no desire to carry too much in his arms and risk a spill, even though under normal circumstances he would have done so. He savoured the aromas from the wines in the glasses as he climbed the stairs, and then walked briskly to the library, setting the glasses on the round table. He then took a bottle of water from the fridge, along with two cheeses, found some crackers, a knife and a small plate, and returned again to the library.

As he did, he took his first sip of the 1999 Burgundy. It was everything he dreamed of, everything he could not afford but desired. It was the wine of the gods and tonight, on his 60th, he would sit amongst them.

Pete began to believe that the stars had created everything for him for this special day: the discovery of the heavenly wines, the absence of both the cook and housekeeper, and the glorious sunset. It was perfect, he thought, as he once again descended the stairs. Gathering the two open bottles and kissing them in turn, he marched back up to the library. "All this exercise is going to kill me," he whispered, winking at the wines.

Pete relaxed into the Chesterfield, opened his notebook, wrote down the two wines he was about to savour and devour and prepared to write his thoughts and reflections on them. He wanted to record these next couple of hours in every detail, even if by the end of the evening he would remember much less!

He found himself detailing not just the aromas he distinctly smelled but also the complexity of taste as the wine flowed from his palate down his throat. He also recorded the memories that came to him as he relaxed and continued to imbibe without a care in the world. Tonight was a night when there would be no house rules and certainly no spitting out of the wine.

As Pete gazed out at the sunset, he topped up his glass and raised it to the sky. Was the universe now intentionally ensuring the sunset matched the red wine?

As yet, the 1975 Domaine de la Romanée-Conti remained untouched, but he could feel the strong pull of wanting to taste it: not just taste it, but get lost in it and be consumed by it.

But despite its reputation, surely it could not be as remarkable as the first? And what if it was even better? Would he return to the first? What a ridiculous dilemma to face – the type he had faced many times when drinking much cheaper wines from little-known vineyards.

Somehow in the midst of thinking all this, he noticed the 1999 Burgundy was already more than half empty. He turned to the cheese and crackers – the night was young and he had no plans to rush paradise.

The grandfather clock chimed 9pm as the first bottle was emptied, and Pete lifted the glass of the 1975 Domaine de la Romanée-Conti, gently swirling the wine in the glass, admiring it, and perhaps adoring it. The bouquet was intoxicating, and Pete could resist no longer, allowing the wine to flow into his mouth. Tonight, he had discovered double perfection as never before.

He made copious notes as he experienced the array of flavours pervading his mouth, enticing him for more, luring him to give in to its hypnotic and sensual powers.

The idea of regret had long since passed. This was the culmination of his life, a wonderful occasion that the universe had planned for him to remind him that, after all, he was special and deserved his moment in time.

He toasted the universe, he raised his glass several times to the gods – even though, beyond Bacchus, he knew very few by name. And with a euphoric sense of benevolence towards all he knew, he toasted his family including his ex-wife, at last able to forgive and let go. Finally, he toasted all his friends and then his wine colleagues. If only they knew. Pete smiled and chuckled again. 'I could get used to this,' he thought to himself.

As he scribbled away between the sheer pleasures of each mouthful, this time comparing the flavours of both, his mobile startled him as it vibrated. The number showed as being from one of the owner's sons. How poignant, he thought. Should he answer and perhaps profusely thank him for the wine he was drinking, without stating which one?

Pete raised his glass as a toast to the sons while the phone continued to vibrate on the small table. Pete was not inclined to take the call, tempting though it was. And then, as he pondered further, the decision was no longer needed as the ringing ceased.

"Your good health," said Pete.

Pete calculated in his mind that since it was now 9pm in the UK, it was 8am the following day in New Zealand – where the sons lived – not a suitable hour for a joint toast at all.

Pete completed his notes and, as he closed his little black

book, the phone rang again. Same number. Pete let it ring again. After all, what a rude interruption this was, unless of course the bereaved son knew it was Pete's birthday. Had he mentioned it? He couldn't remember. Thinking it was possible, Pete reached for the phone, picked it up and said 'hello.'

Mark Abrams was the oldest son and perhaps the smarter of the two. He instantly pitched in: "Hi Pete. Glad you're still awake – I hope I didn't wake you?"

Pete replied: "Not at all, I was just relaxing in your library after another good day's work. I hope that's ok. Such a beautiful room here. I'm certainly on schedule to finish by Friday, as agreed. How's life down under?"

"Well, that's the thing," Mark replied. "I'm actually just back in the UK because we have a buyer for our retail stores, and it's an offer that's too good to refuse. So I'm coming to meet my solicitor tomorrow – he who seems to be making a ton of money out of me in every direction and there's nothing I can do about it."

"Wow," replied Pete. "Congratulations on getting a buyer so quickly. That sounds amazing. So will you get time to drop in?" asked Pete, looking to allay his fears and make plans to cover his tracks. "I mean, I'll select one of your best wines if you want to celebrate in style on Friday – and I can hand over to you then?"

"Actually, Pete, I have some good news for you – that's why I rang. We found the full wine inventory – photos and all. Your life has just been made much easier but don't worry, I will pay you as planned, of course. And since you are still up, I'll give you a copy."

"Great. Thanks so much," bluffed Pete, not quite realising what Mark had meant. "Yeh, just email it to me by the morning and that will help enormously."

"No need," said Mark, "no need at all. I'm actually here now. And you won't believe the special bottles Dad left for us. I was looking through the list on the flight. Remarkable choices." And as he said that, the phone rang off, the library door opened, and Mark bounded in straight up to Pete.

Pete leapt to his feet in a total panic, bumped the round oak table as he did so, and the bottles and glasses fell onto the Persian rug and onto the wooden floor. Pete cursed the universe which had so clearly deceived him. Just as Adam and Eve succumbed to the apple, Pete suddenly knew his downfall was another fruit – grapes. He watched in horror while the two bottles rolled in slow motion along the floor towards Mark's feet.

The Thirty Year Rule
Matthew Coburn

"Believe me, this is bigger than the Watergate scandal."
The woman sounded old, charming, and driven. Probably a
fantasist – if you can say that much about a voice.

"Why me?" As a journalist I normally responded to a
cold call this way.

"I heard about your operation."

"Who the hell are you?"

"It doesn't matter. Just let's not use tweets, skype,
snapchat, or anything like that."

The secretary had put the call through just like any other,
but she said the woman had asked for me by name. 'Ms
Stephanie Ginsberg, please.' My job is to uncover things
that are bigger than Watergate, and I have been trying to do
that for thirty years. My editor's job is to take the glory.
Jack had scooped every story since the Sandinista affair, if
you believed his chat-up lines. My job does not involve
calls about my private life, least of all about confidential
health matters.

"Never mind tweets," I said, "you asked for me by name,
and you mentioned an operation. I already have your phone
tapped and I will see you in court. If you call me again, you
will go to prison."

As I reached for the disconnect button she said…

"Can we start again, please?"

*

We started again, against my better judgement, and we met at a burger joint a few hours later. She wore gloves, as she said she would, but she hadn't mentioned the... I nearly said wheelchair. More like a mobility scooter, but... how can I say this without sounding patronising or prejudiced? Top of the range.

We talked over beef burgers, but she didn't touch hers. I didn't mention the operation. There just didn't seem to be the right moment – but I couldn't sleep that night thinking about her. Not the usual crank, and definitely not the usual snout. No mention of money, and she didn't seem the type to want revenge. I realised as the diazepam kicked in, that we didn't talk about the scandal in detail. She used that word a lot, but in a moral, outraged way. Not normal. She didn't really give me enough information to brief Jack, except calling it the biggest drug deal in history, going right to the top.

*

Next day Jack asked me if I was OK. He's never done that before. My limp is getting worse, but I could normally come to the office with an axe in my head and nobody would notice.

"Yeah, I'm OK. Who's asking?"

"Clarissa."

Our researcher could be the only person in the building who does care about anything, other than their mortgage facility.

"She said you met with Joy McKinlay yesterday. Dr Joy McKinlay."

"For pity's sake, can't a journalist have a beef burger round here without somebody making a story out of it."

"Speak to Clarissa," Jack said, "and get the lowdown - then find me."

*

Clarissa looked startled whenever I spoke to her. Her eyes always glued to her monitor, not allowing any peripheral vision... or so she would have you believe. How, then, did she always have the information that I needed just one click away? She did the research for twenty-five of us, so maybe she had clairvoyant powers.

"Hi Clarissa." I tried to see her tabs on the screen - to check her readiness for me - but she kept some of the tinsel from Thanksgiving over that part of the monitor.

"Oh, Stephanie. How are you? Can I help?"

"Jack sent me over."

"About Dr McKinlay? A very interesting lady. She has been a recluse ever since her husband died. Nobel Laureates, both."

"You know that we could replace you with an algorithm."

"Oh, Stephanie, you're so funny. Anyway, they worked together on diabetes - Type 2. That's when…"

"I know …" Shit. That's too much information. She will realise I have 'Type 2', because ever since I needed a stick she has offered to help me at the water fountain. My excuse that 'I fell over while ice-skating,' got a sceptical flick of her eyebrow, but a polite carefulness not to pry. I quickly corrected myself, "I mean, I know she's a Laureate. What's 'Type 2' diabetes?"

*

"Jack, you said to find you."

"I didn't mean on the crapper, Stephanie."

"Yeah, well, you know what I'm like at finding people."

"Is anybody else in here?"

"How long have you known me, Jack?"

"OK, Stephanie. Joy asked for you by name, so what have you got?"

"The biggest drug deal in history, and it goes right to the top. Bigger than Watergate."

"Ha, ha. You're fired. If you want your job back, you have two days - and I don't want to see beef burgers on your expenses. Now get out of this male toilet facility before I call security."

*

Joy chose to meet me again, 'more properly', while feeding

the ducks in Central Park. Elderly, charming, and driven, just as I first thought from the first phone call. She could have been Clarissa's grandmother, but Clarissa is something out of the Rocky Horror Show. A geek and a freak. On the other hand, Joy exuded the manner of Republican Party royalty: the coat from Bloomingdales, the hat from Harrods, and the spectacles from Paris. Dr Joy McKinlay oozed international fame. I fumbled with Clarissa's notes in my pocket, but I didn't need them:

- Discovered corn sugar with her husband at Harvard in the 1950's.
- Joint Nobels for science in the 1960's.
- Head of the World Health Organisation, the WHO! in the 1980's.
- A recluse since her husband apparently took his own life thirty years ago.
- Nevertheless, still a special advisor on health to the Republican Party.

Joy and Clarissa could both read my mind, and they were both nice. Something about them stuck out in this cynical, frantic metropolis. I am a hack, but I can still see nice when I see it.

"Has your researcher done the science for you yet?" Joy asked.

"Ma'am, I do stories. I need to know why this is a scandal, not just why it's the biggest drug deal in history."

"What if the president hid the truth about the most serious

threat to human health on this planet – and then lied about it."

"Sorry, I don't see a headline. What did Churchill say? The truth is so important it must be surrounded by a bodyguard of lies."

"We've known what causes obesity, heart disease, kidney failure, and diabetes for fifty years. Laura has just put that secret back into the vault at the pentagon."

Is she on first name terms with the president? Or is Laura someone other than President Laura Jackson?

"No sex, lies, or money?" I am not patronising her. She started this, by asking for me by name. I am widely known as the most cantankerous woman on the block.

"Money, yes. Billions. About one twentieth of our Gross Domestic Product."

"OK, how about a headline of 'President 'Poison': Jackson lies to the world'?"

"If you must. Look, I'll be dead soon and you are not far behind me. Do what you have to do." She threw the last piece of bread to the gaggle of birds at our feet. Their frenzy reminded me of the morning meetings, back at the New York Times.

*

Clarissa had done the research on a recent W. H. O. conference. There, President Jackson had laid out her caring credentials to the 'global south' - her name for the developing countries, with most of the world's population. I didn't need it, but Clarissa had also looked for the geeky bit - apparently without success. 'I can't find the science. It looks like it has been buried since the 1970's,' she said. Time to brief Jack anyway, but not at the morning meeting… they are too much of a feeding frenzy. Joy had something, or more likely she was part of something, and she also knew about my operation. The journalist in me straightened. This story had at least enough to sue Dr Joy McKinlay for breaching patient confidentiality. Jack always liked a fallback. An article entitled 'Republicans share patient's notes at party fundraiser' might find its way into the lifestyle section of the paper at the weekend.

Jack agreed to meet me at the strip joint. We're both gay and I don't fancy strippers, but the place pretty much guarantees some privacy - not least because it is too noisy for bugging devices. The girls leave us alone and it doesn't appear on Jack's expenses.

"President 'Poison'. I like the headline. Is it about revenge?" Jack wants an angle.

"I don't think so. You may need another drink before you accept this at face-value, but I think it's about legacy."

"What the hell is that?"

"If you think you're gonna die soon, you want to leave something."

"We're all gonna die soon." He slugs the gin and tonic. "Give me some more on the drug deal… the poison."

"This is not my strong point, but the W. H. O. has declared that sugar is a toxin." He looks at me as if I had just had a stroke. Maybe I have just had a stroke. I am overweight and unfit. In fact, I have the full set of ailments that Joy mentioned: obesity, heart disease, kidney failure, and diabetes… Type 2 - not the family history type. That is probably why Joy called me. ME. Saviour of the world.

"Stephanie, let's do the science another time. Where's the scandal?"

"That's easy. Clarissa no doubt told you that in the 1950's, Joy and her husband discovered how to make sugar from corn. In the 70's they found out this was harmful – I don't know why yet."

"Go on." Jack huffed.

"In the 80's they wanted to brief the W. H. O. but the Pentagon buried that report in the vaults. It's just come up for disclosure after thirty years and Jackson has buried it again. You can only do that for gold-plated national security reasons. Even the hydrogen bomb didn't get put back in the vault."

"You've lost me. Get me the report from the vault, or you're taking a long holiday."

"The point is the president lied about it, only last week at the W. H. O. conference."

"By tomorrow."

*

"Doctor Morland, it's Jack Hargreaves. New York Times."
Phones make Jack nervous.

"I know who you are old chap. Call me Earnest. To what
do I owe this honour?"

"Er… Earnest, you advised Congresswoman Jackson on
health matters during the campaign."

"Jack, I don't think that's a secret."

"I wanted to discuss the corn-sugar report."

A long silence took over, before Dr Morland came back
to the phone.

"You play golf don't you Jack? I have a surgery soon, but
I can see you at the Medina Golf Club later. Let my
secretary know if you need the helicopter. See you later,
old chap."

*

Jack hates golf, and he hates golf buggies even more. The
helicopter and the buggy between them are enough to make
anybody sick, but at least a doctor accompanied him. After
a few holes, Dr Morland brought the conversation round to
Jack's enquiry.

"So Jack, what did you want to discuss?"

"Well, I'll come straight to the point. President Jackson
has just told the W. H. O. that there are no harmful effects
from corn-sugar."

"Jack, old thing, it is not as simple as that. When you are
the first black, female president, and you have only been in

office for a few weeks, well… you rely on your chiefs of staff."

"So she doesn't know about the McKinlays' report, from the 1980's?"

"There is no report."

"At the W. H. O. conference a delegate asked about synthetic sugar, made from the American corn surplus. The president categorically stated that no evidence existed of harmful effects on human health. None."

"Old chap, there are no harmful effects. Ninety per cent of the world's processed food uses it. That's everything you don't eat off a tree, or catch in a trap. Our economy would crash without it. It's been around since the McKinlays made it in a lab in the 1950's. Without it, we would still rely on molasses, cane sugar and sugar beet. Anyway, my dear old thing, the 'bad guy' is fats, not sugars. Your shot I think."

*

"Hi Jack, how was the golf, 'old chap'?" I asked.

"I had to puke in the bunker on the 12th. If you haven't got that report by now, you will be playing a lot more golf than me."

"Not at the Medina. That's for Doctors who provide private health care to the newspaper industry. Anyway, I have something, but they have brought my operation forward to tomorrow. We need to meet this evening. Not at the strip club, somewhere else."

"The office?"

"Ok, but not your office, it's probably wired. Let's use the janitor's cupboard."

*

Clarissa had sprouted roots at her desk. That girl is a diamond, but also a witch. She must know we might need her tonight. I guess she would rather be here with two gays, than go back to her bed-sit, but she looked a bit surprised when Jack and I sneaked into the janitor's cupboard. I jumped out with a mop over my head, and I shouted that there were broomsticks in there for her too. She giggled.

"Jack, Dr McKinlay showed me a copy of the report about the harmful effects of corn sugar, and it's on your desk. They certainly knew how to blind people with science back in the 1980's. The report is for the W. H. O. but it never seemed to get that far."

"Tell me the findings of the report in simple terms."

"Right… when they fed rats with food containing corn sugar, they died of obesity. It just made them hungrier and hungrier. Like an addiction. It's poison."

"How did they know it was the corn sugar?"

"They isolated the sugars and ran control experiments… blah, blah. It's in the report, and you said tell you in 'simple terms'."

"OK. OK. As long as it makes sense to you." Jack

inspected the janitor's coffee cup and sneered at the brown stains inside it. Then, while still looking at the pattern of the stains, he 'saw the light'. "So it's like an addiction - you can't get enough... but because you don't feel you're getting anything." Wow, even I hadn't seen it in those compelling terms. He was on a roll. "Except it's bigger than heroin, cocaine and crystal-meth put together... the corn sugar industry, I mean."

Jack listens to me after all.

"Bingo. But the scandal is that President Jackson lied about it, hence the headline: 'President 'Poison': Jackson lies to the world'. So, I will leave it with you. Can I still get my operation done on the New York Times health scheme?"

"Stephanie, old chap, for ruining America's relationship with the rest of the world, and bringing down the new president, you can also get the rehab on private health care. Who is your surgeon, by the way?"

"Doctor Morland."

*

My eyelids were getting heavy, but I could still just about read Doctor Morland's expression as he leant over me. Not much to go on, with a mask over his mouth and those thick glasses.

"You're with the New York Times, aren't you, Ms Ginsberg?" he asked, probably checking to see if the anaesthetist had got the dosage right.

"Mmmm," I could hardly form the words to say 'yes'.

"I'm very sorry to hear about Jack Hargreave's helicopter accident."

"Mmm? Mmm, mmmmm." My tongue is so heavy, even though it is resting on that spatula that they have shoved into my mouth. "J… J… Joy." I muster all my strength to get my mouth around the sound.

"She will be missed too. She had such a long and fruitful life. Now, we may have to remove some of your functionality, but prosthetics are very good these days."

"Mmmm, mmm, mm, m… ."

*

Clarissa fumbled with the mop head.

"Stephanie was like a mother to me." Placing a picture of me on my desk, next to all the cards, her gothic make-up ran down her face. "Complications? People don't die of complications these days."

The kindly old janitor put an arm round her. "Stephanie was morbidly obese, she even said so herself. It puts a lot of strain on the heart."

Well-wishers had also strewn cards around Jack's office, as well as balloons and flowers. Luckily, Clarissa had found the old-fashioned brown envelope on his desk - marked 'Joy'.

Beyond the Barn

Stephen Young

What earthly impetus is it that drives the moth to the flame? I have sat here now for an age, pen poised above paper, watching just such a creature circle my rapidly diminishing tallow candle before finally immolating itself in spectacular fashion, leaving nothing behind but an acrid smell and tiny blackened carcass. I have had plenty of time to ponder such things since my incarceration in this squalid cell. Four grime encrusted walls have been my only companion until recently, when my repeated requests for pen and paper fell upon sympathetic ears. I must be swift in the transcription of my tale. This may be my only chance to fully document my ordeals before I inevitably succumb to one of the myriad diseases and maladies occupying these walls and the wax of my sole source of illumination is already running low. I suppose it is all too easy to call the moth a fool and move on with it, but I too was drawn by that siren song of curiosity and similarly combusted in spectacular fashion in its flame. I can only hope that this account, scrawled on mottled paper, will reach the hands of one sympathetic to my plight once thrown through the bars of my cell. And if my extenuation is not possible, then at least the finder may know in posterity that, within the squalor of bedlam, Douglas Conrad died an innocent man and a sane man.

As the hay cart trundled down the potholed Devonshire road away from the station, I leaned back against a soft bundle of straw and relished the sense of space following the arduous and cramped journey down from London. A blood-red horizon stretched across the sky as the onset of night started to make itself known and the cawing of gulls filled the salt breeze. Reclined in a state of semi-comfort, I felt the twin pangs of excitation and trepidation. This was the moment I had been waiting for, for so long. An eternity seemed to have passed between my first sighting of the advertisement in the back pages of *The Times* and now. Months of correspondence, meetings with representatives and uncertainty had followed until one morning, when all hope seemed to have gone, a telegram reached my door, requesting that I make myself present at the home of the professor the next day. I had been accepted. After some hasty negotiation with my landlord, and not a little pleading, I settled my affairs, bid farewell to my few friends and set off to the small, coastal town of Byholt.

The town was hardly an attraction in itself but possessed that out of the way charm that a few select locations in England still do. An inn, church and school house all lay within a short distance of the train station before the village became a disperse mess of farm houses and fishing cottages stretching along the coast. I observed all this with casual interest as my humble transport rattled its way past the neatly thatched roofs and smoking chimneys.

Mention the name of Professor Bernard Van Der Stroep now and you will be met with either blank indifference or professional scorn, depending on the company you keep. Indeed, even in my day, he was a figure who courted controversy and resided firmly in the realm of fringe science, despite the soundness and well-meaning nature of his research. This, however, was not always the case. Emigrating to London from his native Leiden in the early 1880s, Van Der Stroep initially garnered huge critical acclaim within academic circles. Pioneering various cutting-edge theories on the nature of sound and light waves, he captivated even lay audiences at his lectures and travelled the length and breadth of the country, combining his flair for showmanship with scientific zeal. Countless universities competed for his fellowship and, to this day, devices bearing signs of his craftsmanship receive frequent use in laboratories on both sides of the Atlantic.

It was at the end of the century that the sterling reputation he had so carefully built up started to crumble. Fabulous claims replaced scientific integrity and his followers dropped off until only an eccentric cadre of obsessives attended his lectures with an almost religious fervour. The good name of Van Der Stroep was smirched and eventually tarnished beyond repair by the press and universities until he entirely dropped off the academic map. Penning only the occasional article for minor journals, nothing was heard of the man for almost a decade. That is, until an advertisement, diminutive and understated, appeared in the personals column of the late edition of *The Times*. "BRIGHT, ENTHUSIASTIC PHYSICS GRADUATE WANTED TO ASSIST IN RESEARCH BY PROFESSOR VAN DER STROEP. COMFORTABLE SALARY AND QUARTERS PROVIDED," followed by contact details, was all the enigmatic message said. To me, this was bait to a very hungry fish.

I was, at the time, living a fairly meagre existence. Following the completion of my studies, I had drifted from one job to the next, the sense of purpose I craved never truly presenting itself. It was on a morning, when, eating my un-buttered toast and dreading the day's torments in the drab firm I happened to be employed in, I stumbled upon the advert. The name was instantly familiar to me. I had been intrigued by the man's work during my undergraduate days and would often pore over his articles with an almost illicit thrill, further heightened by the dismissive manner in which my tutors would mention his name. Whilst I could not have held myself among the ranks of his devotees, the prospect of working for such an elusive and intriguing figure as the professor held an almost boundless sway over me. I knew that I must apply at once.

The cart lurched sideways as a wheel struck a particularly deep rivet and I was shaken from my reminiscence. The stoic donkeys hauling us did not seem bothered, and continued onwards up the path with only a token flogging from the driver of the cart.

"Excuse me sir, but how much further till we reach the house?" I inquired, leaning over the bale.

"Tis not much further, cast your eyes o'er yonder hillock. That there smoke is from the professor's manor," my chauffeur responded in the distinctive drawl of the area. There was indeed a distant wisp of smoke emerging from beyond a hill and I felt comforted by the promise of a warm hearth. The night air was starting to chill my bones and the onset of fatigue had started to creep upon me.

Eventually, we topped the summit of the gentle hill and the rolling countryside behind opened up into a broad ocean vista. There was little wind, and only the smallest of white crests adorned the grey waters that stretched off into the twilight. A fishing vessel, its lanterns already lit and casting a pleasant glow over the surf, was making its way back to land, and the incessant chorus of the gulls grew in volume, as if mourning the loss of the sun. The professor's manor stood atop the cliffs directly ahead. Built entirely out of a sombre, grey brick, the manor was a truly imposing sight in the fading light.

Dense fingers of ivy crept up its three storeys and the rows of windows stood dark and unlit. I gulped. Ever the fabulist, my mind instantly started to conjure up all manner of unsavoury allusions based on this anything-but-inviting looking building. What had I wound myself in? What if the gutter rumours of the tabloid press about this old scientist actually turned out to be true? This impression soon faded though as, upon drawing closer to the old mansion, I became aware of pleasant details I could previously not make out. The lawn surrounding the house was well tended and healthy looking, while neat rows of flowers lined the outer perimeter of the drive. Surely insane occultists, as some of the lower papers claimed the professor to be, did not care for primroses and crocuses.

Finally the cart drew to a rattling halt at the front porch and, alighting from the vehicle, I hauled down my trunk and gave the driver a few coins and muttered words of thanks. With no sign that he had heard me, the wizened man kicked at his steeds and started to negotiate the cart around the turning circle in front of the house. Hauling my luggage to the front door, I paused for a moment, took one very large breath and knocked three times. Only a few seconds had passed before the door swung noiselessly inwards, revealing the slim figure of an elderly oriental man. Dressed in plain but smart garments of his home-land, he held me within his gaze for a split moment, a half smile crossing his lips almost imperceptibly before he finally addressed me.

"Ah, Mr Conrad, I assume. What a great pleasure it is to finally have you here with us in Byholt. I hope your journey was not too unpleasant?" He spoke with perfect Oxbridge enunciation, revealing two immaculate rows of tiny teeth.

"No, no, it was quite comfortable," I lied.

"Well that is a relief. My name is Yao Xiang. I look after the professor and his house, along with assisting in some of the simpler aspects of his research. Here, let me get that." Reaching down, he picked up my trunk, seeming unaffected by its weight. "If you would please follow me. You look like a man who could do with a good meal. I have prepared a light supper which you can take in the dining room." I gladly obliged and followed the surprisingly sprightly old fellow through the door and into the foyer of the house. As I trailed behind, Xiang explained some of the history of the old building culminating in its eventual ownership by the professor. The painted eyes of countless portraits watched as we made our way through a labyrinthine series of corridors until we eventually reached the warmly lit glow of the dining room. I gladly accepted a seat at the end of a long table whilst the elderly Chinaman went to fetch the promised nourishment.

As I wolfed down the hearty meal of venison and potatoes, the manservant sat with me and answered the questions I sent his way. It transpired that the professor was considerably more frail and sickly than I had previously anticipated and spent most of his days either bed bound or in his library reading, only leaving the house very occasionally for a brief constitutional stroll along the coast. Whilst he never explicitly stated it, it was implied by the old manservant that the last decade of negative attention and rancour towards Van Der Stroep by the outside world had taken a major toll upon his health.

"But when might I meet the professor and discuss the nature of the work which we are to undertake together?" I inquired.

"I truly hope that it is not before too long. Professor Van Der Stroep has only today been taken with a fit of weakness and has been prescribed bed rest by his physician. He may well be fit enough to breakfast with you tomorrow morning, but I am reluctant to see him exert himself with his work until the spell has passed." I nodded in agreement and was enthusiastically promised that the surrounding countryside would provide ample diversion until the venerable man was well again.

Having finished my meal and consumed a glass of good red wine, Xiang escorted me from my seat and up two flights of stairs until we reached my quarters. A fire burned snugly in the hearth and inviting sheets lined the generous looking bed. Assuring my host's servant that the room was absolutely adequate, he departed, leaving me to undress and collapse into a deep and dreamless slumber.

Waking up to the sound of the incessant gulls, I drew back the curtains and regarded the gleaming day that greeted me. A perfectly blue sky embraced the ocean and all around the light and optimism of spring glowed. Casting my eyes across the sprawling grounds, I noticed a building

I had not seen the previous night. A squat barn with a thatched roof stood parallel to the manor and outside all manner of boxes and containers lay strewn. Paying this little regard, I washed, dressed and made my way downstairs, trying to recollect my path from the hazy memory of the last night. Eventually I reached a corridor lined with portraits which seemed more familiar than the others. It was then that I heard raised voices coming from behind a door.

"Doctors be damned, I tell you I am as fit and well as I ever have been. Time waits for no man: I shall meet with this Conrad on this very morning so that we can commence our work as soon as is possible."

"But professor, I think it is highly advisable that you…"

"Highly advisable? Damn it, man, I don't hire you to advise me. I am set on the matter. Now if you please, my breakfast!"

Ascertaining this unfamiliar voice to be that of Professor Van Der Stroep, I felt an inward rush of excitement. Pushing the door open, the dining room of last night was revealed and I saw the manservant, mouth open, presumably pre-retort. Noting my arrival, he clamped his mouth down, gave a low bow and turned on his heels, leaving me alone with the figure I could now see seated opposite. Cocooned within a plush looking bath robe sat the bony figure of the professor. Only a few sparse strands of grey hair still adhered to his wrinkled head, yet his face was one of cunning intelligence.

"Good morning, my boy! I hope that our little altercation has not left you perturbed. Yao is one of the best companions a man could hope for in his old age - reliable, loyal and a fine chef to boot. Yet he does seem to care for my health a trifle too zealously. Please do take a seat, we have so much to discuss. Do you take tea? I happen to have here a fine blend I stumbled upon during a former sojourn through Indo-China."

I assented and took a seat facing the man whilst he poured me a cup of the heady smelling brew.

"Now I am sure that you have all sorts of questions you are burning to ask and I assure you that they will all be answered in due course, but if you would permit an old man the luxury of a brief monologue, I would be most grateful." I gestured my consent and took a tentative sip of the tea, finding its taste surprisingly subtle.

"I do not know to what extent you are aware of my life's work and discoveries and, to be honest, it really matters very little at this point. In fact, it was partially for that exact reason that I chose you for my task over the horde of sycophants who would still leap like a trained spaniel at such a chance." A look of slight contempt flitted across his face before vanishing.

"For the last fifty five years, I have been dedicating my research to the investigation of the two most fundamental forces which guide our perception of the universe: light and sound. Through careful manipulation and observation, I have, to varying degrees of success, been able to alter their core properties, creating all sorts of curious phenomena. This was all before your time, of course, but I was regarded in some circles as something of a conjurer, albeit one with a penchant for total scientific transparency in his methods. All that seems like another life ago now. Since my well documented fall from public grace, I have turned my attention from the theoretical to the applied. It is now my heartfelt belief that not only does our limited sensory input define our perception, but also our very physiological make-up."

"This is not the time or place to expound to you the extent of my theory, but let it suffice for now that the next few weeks have the potential to shake so called 'modern' science to its core. I have created blueprints for a device which will, if I am not mistaken, prove my hypothesis without a shadow of a doubt. This is where you come in. I lack the physical strength to actualise this creation and Yao does not have the technical knowledge. Your role here will be to combine the brawn and brains which Yao and I lack collectively, to piece together the device to my exact specifications. I hope this does not seem too disagreeable to you?"

I was taken aback. I suspected that the old professor may be slightly unhinged, but this was more than I could possibly have anticipated.

"I... I... I really don't know. Your ideas, they sound fabulous to say the least."

"Please do not stutter: it is something I cannot abide. I did not ask you for your judgement on my theory. Your opinion of it is irrelevant to the project at hand. I merely asked if you were willing to construct my device for me. It is well within your capabilities. You stand to lose nothing, yet gain potentially everything."

"No sir, I mean professor, I understand. Yes, I would be most happy to assist in your, um, project. I just don't quite understand the full implications of what you are saying." A broad, honest smile illuminated the man's face.

"Do not worry on that account my lad, very soon you will. Now, come, we have no time to lose. The schematics are in my study, please follow me."

Rising precariously from his chair, the professor led me out back into the corridor, the prospect of breakfast suddenly forgotten. His study only lay a few yards down the hall and I was excitedly ushered in. The room was softly furnished; the remains of last night's fire smouldered in a hearth and three bookcases of monolithic proportions lined the walls. The only item perhaps out of place in a study of an elderly academic was a small print of Blake's *Ghost of a Flea*, hanging above the most central shelf. Even in the gently lit study, the great romantic's grotesque image, all otherworldly muscle and fangs, did not fail to elicit a slight shiver in me.

Upon the central desk lay a large tube of black lacquered wood. Taking it in his hands, Van Der Stroep turned to me with pride in his eyes.

"This is it, the sum culmination of years of suffering and pain. My *magnum opus* if you would forgive such a bold statement. The contents herein are to become your bible over the coming days. Study them, learn them and make them a reality. I place a lot of trust in your hands; please do not let me down."

Taking the vessel from him, I turned it over in my hands and contemplated its heft. This would be no small undertaking.

"I have a barn not too far from the main building. This is where I want to build my creation. All the components are here and I have provided the finest tools and materials money can buy. If you do not mind, I would like you to begin at once; I have waited so long for this moment to finally arrive."

The professor suddenly looked wearied. Collapsing in an armchair, he looked very old. There was a slight noise behind me and I turned to see the slim figure of the manservant appear in the open doorway.

"Yao will show you to the barn now. I fear that I have got myself quite worked up and may need a few moments' repose. I shall check in with you later on in the day. Please do not be afraid to go to Yao if there is anything at all you need." Sinking deeply in his chair, the professor gave a small sigh and closed his eyes. Turning back to the man in the doorway, I felt a small amount of pity towards Van Der Stroep. What a tragedy it was to see such an esteemed man turn towards such lunatic schemes. The public could be such a blindly cruel force and I wondered if his detractors would regret their character assassinations if they could now see what a pitiful figure they had created.

Mr Yao led me in silence through the building and out of a back door. I did not really mind. I had too many thoughts galloping around my mind to engage in conversation. Crossing a neat yard, we reached the barn. It was simple in design and manufacture but spacious looking and sturdy. Outside it, I saw the crates I had previously noted from my bedroom window. Up close, I was taken aback at the sheer enormity and variety of the gathered packages. Shipping labels in Russian, Mandarin and numerous other foreign scripts lined the cases which ranged from short and flat to tall and curved. The Chinaman weaved through these boxes before unbarring the door, swinging both doors inwards at once. Inside, the barn was barren. Not even a single cobweb was to be seen throughout the whole building.

"Well Mr Conrad, I am sure that you have much to be getting on with. Should you require anything, you can find me in the house."

Bidding him farewell, I stepped into the barn. The outside warmth instantly vanished, giving way to a cold sterility. Remembering the tube in my hands, I removed the lid and slid out the contents. Inside was a thick roll of heavy paper. Finding no suitable surface, I emptied it on the floor, spreading out the document, covering a large area of the ground in front of me. Gasping, I took in a first impression of the blueprints. Covering the paper in a spider-like mesh was the most complex series of diagrams I had ever laid eyes upon. This was the last shred of proof I needed. The professor was most undoubtedly insane. Training my eyes, I followed line upon line, converging and entangling in what seemed an infinitely complex series of patterns. A tiny, neat script annotated all over, whilst a key provided a monumental list of squiggles and patterns within one corner. Despite my conviction that the creator of such a document must be incurably mad, I sat there and persisted, tracing the precise etches until my head spun.

When Mr Yao eventually came in with lunch, I was no further on in my study of this arcane looking diagram and had come to feel a simultaneous mix of awe and fear at the sole mind who had created such a monstrosity. I continued in this manner without making a single step of headway, when at five o'clock, as the outside light was beginning to fade, I suddenly felt an inkling of understanding creep over me. Yes, the man was still mad, but there was definitely a method to it all. Feeling exhausted, but energised by my minor breakthrough, I retired to the manor where a meal of liver and onions was awaiting me. Despite his promise, the professor did not make himself present and I ate alone before returning to my bedroom to dream dreams of strangely flitting filamentary patterns.

The next two weeks continued in much the same way. Bit by bit, I found myself comprehending progressively more of the diagrams until I eventually found the confidence to haul into the barn a few of the crates. Prising them open with a crowbar, I found all manner of bizarre sections of metal, glass and wire. To my relief, every one of these strange components corresponded to a symbol in the key and before too long I had constructed the rudimentary shell of the machine.

All this time, I had seen no sign of the professor and my questions pertaining to his absence were met with vague replies from his manservant until, one evening, returning to the manor's dining room exhausted after the day's labours, I found him sitting in the same chair I had first met him in. We talked superficially on the matter of the project. He seemed distracted and I was too worn out to offer much in the way of conversation and, before long, our already stilted dialogue wore out and we continued eating in silence. Finishing before me, he set down his cutlery and reclined back, fixing me in a cold stare.

"I have something to show you which I hope may be of some interest." Without waiting for a response, he rose before turning to the door. Leaving my meal unfinished, I too left my seat and followed, chewing the remainder of my mouthful.

We trailed down the hallway, the thin light of the gas lamps casting provocative shadows behind us, and the dark countenances of the portraits staring resolutely into space.

Eventually we reached a room of which I had yet to see the interior. Turning a large key, the professor turned to face me. "This room serves as my laboratory. Every one of my discoveries and insights within the last decade was made within this room and I must ask that you treat it with the same respect as you would a chapel. It is my sanctuary from the cold, uncaring world outside."

Struggling to find the words to answer this odd request, I merely nodded dumbly. Pushing the door open, we entered. Work benches lined each wall, some supporting delicate looking devices of copper and glass, others with microscopes and the precision tools needed in dissection. A bookshelf to our right contained ten or eleven large glass jars, each containing meticulously prepared lateral sections of a human brain suspended in formaldehyde. It was through these that the gas lamp shone, bathing the whole room in a sickly yellowish glow and dispersing otherworldly shadows across the walls. It felt as if we had entered into a room belonging to a dream, such was the uncanny effect of the lighting upon the scene.

In the very centre of the room lay a sort of plinth, and upon it a glass box containing what appeared to be a mechanical device. Walking in further to inspect the object, a wave of shock passed over me. I recognised the spindly metal structure supporting the machine: it was that of the creation in the barn! Inside the outer shell, a delicate mesh of threads and wires wound obliquely, intertwining and looping like a distorted image of a harp or some other stringed instrument, though its complexity put to shame the work of any luthier. Hanging from various strings was an array of objects including a range of minute bells and an ampoule of a swirling, noxious looking vapour. So this was the object that I had been tasked with building. Totally absorbed in this incredible lunatic contraption, I did not notice the professor joining my side.

"So I see you have found my device. I created this model some years ago. Compared to the blueprints I have given you, this is a crude, rudimentary prototype, but it does work to an extent. I have seen some of its effect on rodents and other small mammals, but the machine I have tasked you with constructing, I hope, will be a bit more human sized." I spun and stared at him with horror. His eyes softened and he gave a kindly smile.

"Oh please, do not look quite so alarmed. It really is not as bad as it sounds. Please don't think of me as some Victor Frankenstein character till you know the true purpose of the machine. Come, let me explain something to you."

We turned away from the device in the box and walked over to one of the walls where the rows of brain slices hung suspended in preserving fluid.

"Please turn your eyes to this particular specimen. It once

belong to a Hindu monk, or sadhu as they are called over there, who, whilst incapable of speech, seemed to have the uncanny ability of being able to accurately sketch images of the dead relatives of strangers merely through touch. Word travelled, and he eventually developed a loyal band of worshippers who would come from miles around to witness this miracle and lay hands upon him. Unbeknownst to his followers was that, for the first twenty years of his life, this fellow was held captive by a particularly barbarous and devilish death cult. For a full twenty years he was subjected to certain stimuli in the hope that he could one day become their captive seer or prophet. Imprisoned in their basement cell in Bombay, all this monk was permitted to hear for two decades was the thin wailing of ceremonial flutes and the chanting of the cultists until, one day, he escaped. The cruelty of the cultists is undeniable, but their actions have served to provide me with irrefutable proof to my theorem.

"Please take a look at this sample here. See this structure, protruding up from the hippocampus? I have dissected countless brains and I have never, never seen such a formation. I do not believe it to be a tumour but some auxiliary appendage, grown following the repeated exposure to just the right sort of auditory stimulation that has permitted him to develop sensory powers beyond those of our own. Just consider it, Conrad, what if the mystics, sages and seers of history had not been blessed with supernatural powers, but had merely been born with select physiological differences that had permitted them to see beyond the veil that we in our limited understanding call reality? I am certain that this is the case and, with my machine, I intend to prove it."

The professor had worked himself to a fever pitch of excitement, bringing his fist down into his cupped hand with a thump as he emphasised his last point.

"If you are right, then you really are onto the discovery of the century, but you'll forgive me if I withhold my final judgement. The claims you are making are just too fabulous for me to take in at this moment. But I still don't understand, where does the device come into all this?"

"Ah, the device. The crux upon which all this rests. What the abhorrent cultists did to the poor sadhu in twenty years, I intend to do to myself with the assistance of the device in twenty minutes. My creation shall create a sustained frequency, one which I have spent years calculating and perfecting, which is to be beamed through certain vaporous substances until it has taken on absolutely specific characteristics. Once this is so, the tone will be directed into my ears, altering my core brain structure and hopefully granting me perceptions hitherto unknown to sane minds."

I was stunned. The tabloids were right. The fusty academics were right. Professor Van Der Stroep was well and truly cracked. The very core basis of his hypothesis was insane enough on its own, but to believe that he could induce some sort of extrasensory power in himself was beyond all reason. Once again, I looked down on this diminutive, withered old man and felt a deep sense of pity and sadness.

"Do you believe in God, Conrad?" The question took me by surprise and I had to take a moment to compose an answer.

"I suppose I do in a sort of abstract sense of the term. Obviously I don't go in for any of that interventionist mumbo jumbo, but I have always felt that the world seems to be run on some sort of cosmic order."

He looked disappointed by my answer. "Yes, I suppose that I would have probably said something similar at your age. I'm going to be totally honest with you, Conrad. I'm dying. I may look strong enough now, but I can assure you that the majority of my time is spent in agony. My doctors seem to disagree on the matter, but the general consensus is that this is going to be my final year on this earth. I have solved a great many riddles about this material realm during my lifetime, yet absolutely none about what comes next. I am just as in the dark as you or any other human on that matter. All I want now, more than anything else, is to find just a shred of evidence that something exists beyond all this, a single scrap of proof that everything I have travailed over in this life has not been for naught. If my device provides a means of doing so, then I shall not hesitate in embracing the opportunity. Do you now understand the enormity of your task here?" In that gloomy laboratory, he gripped my arm in a cold vice of a grip. A bead of sweat rolled down my forehead as we maintained intense eye contact for almost a minute.

Not much more was said after that. Whilst my conviction that the professor was deranged now felt sadly validated, my determination to complete the device and perhaps provide a shred of solace to an old dying man was stronger than ever. The next morning I set about my work with increased gusto.

For the next month, I laboured in the barn until, eventually, I felt an intimate level of understanding towards the schematics despite still not fully understanding the workings of the device. One by one, the complex threads I had seen in miniature in the laboratory that night were stretched across the barn, from rafter to generator, to resonance chamber and back again to rafter until the whole room began to resemble the work of a disorientated spider. During this month, I saw no sign of the professor and I began to feel afraid that he would not live to see the completion of his final creation. It was with great relief that I found the professor one morning sitting in his usual chair, taking breakfast. He looked visibly older since my last sighting of him and he sat slumped with a tragically geriatric air. Yet when he noticed my entrance, I saw that none of the light had died in his eyes. Yao came in bearing a plate of eggs and we talked as I ate.

"So how goes the project? Please accept my apologies for not checking in on you more frequently. My health has taken a turn for the worse and the slightest exertion saps my energies these days."

"Please don't be sorry. I have managed quite well in your absence. I am almost near completion now. All that remains is the connection of the main generator and the insertion of the gasses into their flasks. Hopefully all should be finished by tomorrow evening if I have correctly interpreted your diagrams." The professor beamed broadly and years dropped off his apparent age.

"I am so very pleased to hear that. It appears that you have really got to grips with the device and its inner workings. Once it is fully operational, I have one last request of you. If you have no objections, I would like you to help me into its central auditory chamber and record for posterity's sake your observations of its initial run. I know you remain sceptical and won't bring any unwanted bias into your data. If I have been misguided, then you can return home, well financially reimbursed, but, if not, you shall secure your place in the annals of scientific progress." Curiosity burning within me, I agreed and finished my breakfast.

As predicted, the device was finally completed the following day. I dined with the professor that night and we drank a whole decanter of expensive tasting brandy between us as he excitedly recounted tales to me of his past life and exploits. I found myself hardly listening. What if, despite all the odds, the professor's theories turned out to be true? What would I see in that barn the next day? For the first time, a sliver of fear entered me.

A grey sky blanketed the following morning. The threat of rain hovered in the air and an overwhelming sense of atmospheric pressure was all around. As arranged the last evening, I found the professor in the barn at around seven o'clock. Seated in a bath chair, he sat reclined, gazing up in a state of childlike joy at the device. Finally, he turned to look at me.

"By God, Conrad, you've done it. This is my master work made flesh. Can you imagine how it feels, to see an idea you have obsessed over for years finally made reality?" He gave one of the threads a slight pluck and a low note spread wave like throughout the barn. He closed his eyes and let out a slight hum, in tune to that emanating from the strings and wires spread out in front.

"I first heard this note in a dream, you know. It was revealed to me by my own sleeping mind, if you would believe that." He sat in quiet enjoyment of the sound, before snapping out his revelry with an intense start.

"The time has come, Conrad. If you please, shut the door and wheel me into the central chamber." I pushed the bath chair through the narrow tunnel, through the meshing wire until we reached the place where an ornate looking crown dangled from the ceiling. Two brass domes on either side of the headset apparatus connected to two separate bell jars held pendulum like from a crossbeam, ominous grey-green gas swirling in each.

The professor gave me one last smile and, taking the metal and leather protuberance, placed it over his head, perfectly cupping both ears and leaving only the eyes and mouth visible.

"Now Conrad, to the primary generator. I have been ready for this for a long time. I need no further delays." Not giving myself a chance for any second guessing, I proceeded to the large generator standing by the main door. "Pull the lever, Conrad, and don't forget to record everything and anything I say. We're making history here, boy." Grasping the lever in both hands, I yanked it downwards. Almost instantly, the faint note I had heard earlier started rippling around the room. Like the ripples following the dropping of a pebble in a pond, the whole room began to rumble. It was a sickly sweet sound, completely unlike any I had ever encountered, yet somehow maddeningly enticing. I could see the seated man clearly through the mess of strings and his smile was beaming brighter and brighter by the second. Eventually, the hum died down and all that was left was a rhythmic pulsing of the gas in the vials.

"My God, it's beautiful. Not a single earthly composer has ever created such a sublime sound," the professor called out, ecstasy transforming his voice. "If you could

127

hear it as I could!"

I briefly felt a pang of envy. Why should he be the one to experience the sole pleasure of the device? Did I not build it, after all? This was my creation as much as his. But I dutifully continued to document his words.

About five minutes had passed and the professor had ceased all communication. The bizarre dance of the churning gas and the low rumble of the generator was my only company in those tense moments of anticipation. Suddenly, the professor stuck out his arm, grasping at the air. "Colours, I can see colours, Conrad. Colours I have never seen before. They're beautiful, they're... Argh! How can one begin to describe sight to a blind man? Our own light spectrum seems like a drab thing in comparison. If only you could see!" He laughed and continued to wave his hands in front of his body, seemingly manipulating something unseen.

"What's this now? 'Colours' barely begins to describe them. They have voices, Conrad; they're singing to me. What music. What incredible majesty. Are these angels? They're moving all around me now, they know my name. No, not angels, these entities are beyond such base definition. Words couldn't possibly begin to define them. No, please stay, I have so much to learn from you, please!" He implored the empty air, snatching at the space like a child. I looked up from my note taking and saw a change occur in the suspended bell jars. The pulsing gave way to a frantic throbbing as the gas mottled in colour to an even sicklier hue. The professor fell silent for a moment before his smile started to fade.

"What? No! Don't show me that, for the love of God, please don't show me that." The throbbing intensified, growing more violent.

"Oh Jesus Christ, please! Conrad, man, can't you see them? Of course, you can't. They're all around you, they're all over everything. I can see them flitting, passing through the spaces between spaces! To think that we walk around, conduct our lives without the smallest awareness that THEY are among us! It's too ghastly to bear. Arrrhhhh!" He let out a high pitched wail as his eyes rolled back in their sockets. The frail old man started convulsing grotesquely. Strange syllables spewed from his mouth in a voice which was not his own.

"Iah Iah, Nyarlathothep f'tagn, Dagon f'tagn, Iah Iah!" These words grew louder and more inhuman as the man writhed and contorted his limbs into obscene and unnatural postures. Then, through the chaos and noise, I heard the old man scream in a voice which was once again his own.

"Please! Conrad, make it stop, save me from this!" I rushed forward, stumbling on the uneven flagstones as I ran. The professor had started intoning his garbled mantra once more in that fearful voice as I sped through the tunnel into the central chamber. Up close, the sight of this wretch was almost more hideous than I could handle. Digging deep for a pocket of reserve, I persevered onwards, wrenching the headset from the professor and lifting him out of his bath chair. He was a greater dead weight than I had anticipated. As I struggled to catch my balance, my foot caught on the chair, sending the two of us flying into one of the large jars which now churned with a violent intensity. With a great crash, it shattered. In a flash, the barn vanished from sight. In its place, the swirling void of outer space encircled all the eye could see. All around us, nameless creatures heaved and shuddered nebulously, stroking our faces with long, thin tentacles. I felt a scream leave my mouth as my sanity was torn asunder.

Fighting to stay conscious, I looked up through the twisting entities and saw the hem of a tattered yellow robe flapping against pale, bony legs. Gazing upwards, I saw a face looking down upon me with a cold, sardonic hatred I never thought possible in human form. Crowned with a diadem of purest obsidian and with high, regal cheekbones, stood before me a king, ancient beyond comprehension and with eyes burning with malicious intent. As a hot wind blew, the robe fluttered open, revealing a horrific vista. In its blackness, I saw the destruction of all order, the enslavement of mankind and the cataclysmic death of the universe. Reeling, I feebly clutched at the hem of the king's pallid gown as he slowly turned and walked away. As consciousness left me, I could see the distant shape of the barn door open and the low form of the monarch, suddenly clad in earthly clothes, leave into the morning light.

When the police entered the barn, there was not a lot for them to go on. The device lay around us in ruins, and the professor, whose body I was discovered upon, was dead. The next months passed by in a haze of unreality. No trace of Yao could be found and the manor had burned to the ground, leaving behind only a smouldering carcass. There was no trial and, although no weapon or motive could be found, I was incarcerated for the murder of Professor Van Der Stroep with little deliberation.

This is my sorry tale, exactly as it happened. I know I am not insane. If you are reading this, then I implore you, do not forget about me, though I am beyond all redemption. Horror beyond words was unleashed upon the world that fateful morning and all my warnings have so far been interpreted as the ravings of a lunatic. The world needs to know that it is not safe whilst the king in yellow walks it. I have seen his plan for earth and I pray that outside these walls, someone knows how to stop it.

Intolerance

David Lawrence

I drew up one of the three chairs at the end of the table and began my breakfast, a piece of pork and two eggs. That was the last food I had, except for a basket of berries that were just starting to go off, meaning a foray to the woods very soon. The coffee went down well and revived my sagging spirits.

I checked Pa's old timepiece. It was 9:30. I pushed my plate and mug to one side and turned my attention to the arsenal of weapons laid out across the oaken refectory table. Two Navy Colt revolvers, commandeered in '65 when the brigades were disbanded, each with a round in every chamber and two knives; one an old dirk my grandfather gave me from the old country and one an army bayonet. The breech-loading rifle that would accommodate the bayonet was propped up against the table. I spent the next hour or so dismantling, oiling and removing all traces of rust, neglect or damage to the working parts of the guns.

I wiped the gun oil from my hands with an old rag which I threw into the trashcan under the tin basin. I reloaded both guns, spinning the chambers, relishing each satisfying click. I returned the can of gun oil to the bottom of the oak dresser against the back wall and glanced at Pa's old timepiece affixed to my waistcoat pocket. It was around

10:45 and already the cabin was warming up.

I was agitated. The fingers of my left hand ran along the razor edge of the bayonet. This kind of waiting puts a strain on a man's constitution. There was no respite even if I allowed my mind to wander. It was always there, like a ticking clock. It makes your guts crawl and the nights and days long. It torments the soul, just wondering. Your imagination turns over how they will come for you, the consequences, the finality of it all. Perhaps that was their game. It was day three. It seemed longer.

I carried my tin mug over to the stove where I refilled it and went to the south-facing window and opened it slightly. The inrush of fresh air revitalised the cabin. I could just make out the valley below through the tall grasses and wild flowers that even now played host to butterflies and one or two hornets. It was the sort of morning that draws a man outside for a day in the saddle or working the land. It was a good, hopeful day.

I retrieved my army field glasses to take a better look, adjusting the focal length to try and make out the road that left the town, but it was just too far away to make out movement. I put them down, realising that this would be too open for a full frontal assault. I went across to the east-facing window above the tin basin where the oaks at the edge of the wood provided a shady backdrop to the sun-drenched grasslands surrounding the cabin. The road from the town ran across the south-east edge of the woods before dipping down to run along the foot of the valley beside the river. This would be the direction they would come.

I continued my recce, checking my defences. I shot back the bolts and removed the bar, opening the door a fraction and then completely, keeping it between my body and the woods. I anticipated sharp shooters training their sights, waiting for a moment of carelessness. The hairs on the back of my neck were crawling. From within the cool of the cabin I stooped down without stepping onto the veranda and examined my defences. I had strung a cord of twine along the front of the cabin, some ten feet away and some thirty feet long with tin cans, pots and pans and all manner of metallic kitchenware acting as clappers that would bang and rattle the pots if anyone so much as touched the cord. Of course, if they came from behind or during the day I would have no such warning and they would secure an easier victory. No matter, it was all I could do in the time I thought I had. The sun was just breaking over the tallest of the trees and the air was fresh to the touch. It smelled of dry earth and heat.

I closed the door. I put the bar in place and shot the two bolts. The cabin was the old family home, big enough for four although it had been some time since it had been so blessed. I had done all I could to keep things tidy, what else was there to do? It's the way Jess always kept things. Curtains and cloths, knick-knacks and pictures we'd collected along the way. The adze-marked log floor had been swept every day. I instinctively straightened an old sentiment framed on the wall above the stove embroidered in Jess's mother's tight stitch.

I went back to the refectory table and took the rifle, bayonet and shells, and brought them to the south-facing window, propping the long iron barrel against the sill and placing the bayonet and shells along the narrow ledge. If they did come from this direction I would need a long range weapon. My rifle had served me well and I had returned it to its original glory. Although no match for the new repeaters, I had become quite the marksman. Load, fire, eject, load, fire, eject, and make every shot count.

I continued my rounds like a captain checking his troops before battle, lifting morale and searching for weakness. In the bedroom I looked west toward the barn and the open space in between what daddy had called the "yard" with the water pump and trough. The barn would make ideal cover for an assault. The aspect of the large room cast it in shade with the big bed and the two chests of drawers and a couple of side tables. As children we used to come in here and play with our toys as soon as the sun was up. Daddy used to curse us for waking him but I don't think he really minded. He was a good man, strong and open

Jess had laughed so much when I built the bed, knowing how lousy I was with a hammer and nails, but I did it and we agreed they would have to use dynamite to break it apart if we ever moved. I fingered the bedspread we had made, embroidering long into the night. We were neither of us against turning our hands to such things. I could embroider as well as Jess could tote a gun. I would read my books in the rocking chair beside the stove and smoke my briar. I confess that now, even the aroma of my tobacco brings me low. Jess would look at me as I was reading and say "Boy, you're a handsome devil. You know that?" and I would say "dang right I am an' don't you forget it."

Memories crowded in and weighed me down like a bale of hay until I sat down on the edge of the bed where I had not slept since my return. I had kept all night vigils in the rocking chair directly in front of the cabin door, nursing my rifle and catching a few scraps of sleep here and there. But sleep didn't come easy. What does a man do when he's at his wits end with little to say and no-one to say it to. My senses were alert to the slightest tell-tale sound of approaching danger. It gnaws on your bones until you crave release by any means at all. I lay back and stared at the ceiling. How often we had lain here. My body ached with exhaustion and I'm not ashamed to say with …fear. I could just as easily turn my face down into the counterpane and let go and to Hell with whatever came through the door.

I suddenly awoke and sat up. I checked the timepiece and it was gone 11:35. That was foolish. I should be armed. Always armed. If they come without warning through the side or the back, I cannot be caught here, dozy and slow. I went back into the living room. I went to the Colts, one mine and one Luke's. Mine was the least battered. He never seemed to be able to take care of anything. I couldn't help smile at the times he and I would practice our quick draw like those characters from the Penny Dreadfuls. I became pretty good but my kid brother, he'd catch the edge of the holster and the gun would spin out of his hand. My God, that boy was more a danger to himself than any bushwacker. As it turned out, he never got the chance to even pull the trigger.

I picked up mine and felt its reassuring weight in my right hand. I wasn't a bad shot as it turned out but these old war horses were notoriously inaccurate. They were made for close quarter combat. I'd seen a lot of men brought low, gut shot to die in agony and bleed out. Most deaths I saw were from untreated wounds that drive a man to his grave, taking a tortuous road through hell before the final release. The only quick kill was the head shot that would blow a man's skull in half. I prayed that when my time came, the one pulling the trigger would know how to shoot. I tucked my Colt into my belt and stuck the dirk in my boot. There was room and I'd seen this trick before. Always handy in a tight corner.

I checked the stock room that used to be mine and Luke's bedroom. It had a small high up window we could never see out of. It was cool and me and Jess had called it the larder which is where I kept a basket of berries and some cuts of pork, and provisions. Now all I had was the berries and a few grains of coffee. It seemed so long since I was able to just ride into town trouble free, just to stock up. Hell, who was I kidding? It was never trouble free, but it was never like this.

I noticed that the wooden pail was low on water so I picked it up and lugged it out. It meant a trip to the pump. I decided to delay until I needed to drink. Anyway, would it be so bad to just be picked off by some long-range bushwacker? I'd never know and it would end all... this. But my soul continued to burn. Survival is in-built even for a man like me with nothing left to lose. Suddenly, every-day routines seem precious. I'd heard men say as much about war. It was the most alive they had felt. I don't agree. Living in hell may be interesting but it's still hell! I sat for a while in the old rocker, which was permanently positioned squarely in front of the cabin door. The first man through would get no further.

I checked the timepiece at 12:45. It was time to eat. It was always time, when there's nothing else to do. Strange that I had now developed an appetite despite having none when I arrived. I think my body knew it must build up its strength. I went back to the store room and took a handful of the berries. They were definitely going off, but I screwed up my face and devoured a handful. The bitterness almost made me retch.

I needed more than this. I'd had sufficient provisions for the first day and a half. I don't think I expected to be still up here. On the first night I had sat in the rocker, rifle in hand, afraid to fall asleep, although I'm sure I did. I had given real consideration to riding into town and collecting what I needed at gun point, but they would be waiting and some young chancer would try and make a name for himself. Ol' Pa Tunstall had a ranch close on a mile away but he was no sympathiser of mine and even if he were he'd no more give me aid than shoot himself in the head. His sons would have brought hell down on him for aiding a man such as me. No, I just had to sit things out here.

I cursed the day my horse had run off. She had been in the old barn out back since the first day and night, but sometime that night she had gone. But the more I thought things over the more I decided that she had not run. One of them Tunstall boys had been up here and had ridden her off. If they could get so close without disturbing me I had to set something to give me warning, which was when I'd set my trip wire and the pots and pans orchestra.

Now here I was, trapped, unless I decided to set out on foot, but I had become tired of running. It was no way to live and the cost had already been more than any man should have to bear. This time things would be brought to a close, even if they broke open the door and found me dead through hunger.

I had ridden here like the wind itself, dismounting expecting them to be hard on my heels like a pack of dogs. But their self-righteous zeal must have deserted them for no one had followed, or at least no one I could see. Perhaps they expected to meet more than my guns. It wouldn't surprise me if they hadn't sent Comanche Joe to keep watch. I knew I would never see him.

Without an immediate fight I had settled into an uneasy routine of survival, preparation, eating and sleeping and staying close to the cabin. I knew and I guess they knew that I would be self-sufficient here for a few days. Maybe they figured I would cut and run once the food ran out and pick me off, caught in the open. But why wait for that? I'm trapped here like a rat in a trap. Why not take me here? If I didn't know them better I'd say they were hell-bent on shredding my nerves, but in my experience a mob is usually unburdened by strategic thinking.

The day drew on like a cougar stalking its prey. On arrival, the certainty of an immediate confrontation had kept me in a state of constant alert. That first morning I had dragged one of the chairs out onto the porch and I had sat there, rifle in hand, with my eyes on the woods. Me and a rifle, shaded from the rising sun by my old army hat and the cool shadow of the veranda. No one came. That afternoon I had collected some berries, freshened up, ate a little and even dozed off for a few minutes out on the porch. The night found me keeping my rocking chair vigil and the following day I decided to stay inside.

Both nights I had trained my field glasses out of the south-facing window looking for torch bearers in the valley below. I watched the warm glow of house lights burning in parlours and on porches and thought of the folks going about their business, drinking, whoring, raising kids, the shopkeepers and gamblers and the old folk on the porches wishing they were young. They were not all bad people. Some I had even thought of as friends. Good folks, just looking for a new life, seeing the best in whatever life put their way. And yet their benevolence nurtured the shameless souls who would blame anyone including the devil for the sins they commit. Voices would be raised in hatred with the self-righteous conviction of the morally bankrupt. And here I am, the object of so much intolerance? But I knew why, especially in the light of what I'd done and how weak the law was.

At 2:15, I went into the bedroom, and surveyed the "yard" and the pump that had been our lifeblood ever since we'd made our way up here. The spring that daddy had divined was something we had always kept to ourselves but I do recall Ol' Pa Tunstall sniffing around wondering if we was willing to sell up. He saw the location was a prime one, given its proximity to liquid wealth. But daddy said he was staying put, which we knew put us in harm's way, but no harm came. I always felt Tunstall was a little bit afraid of daddy because of his schooling. He never got used to the way he would use words the old rancher never knew. Maybe Tunstall even respected him a little for what he'd achieved. A man of means speaks the same language as another cut from the same cloth. Anyways, we stayed and no one tried to take what was rightfully ours.

The sun was passed its zenith and I decided the time was now. I put on my old army hat, unbolted and unbarred the cabin door and, with the pail in one hand and my Colt in the other, slipped outside. Keeping to the shadows and with one eye on the oaks I stepped around to the side of the cabin and then round the back to the pump beside the water trough. I stooped down looking for the tell-tale flash of a sniper's sights. I listened to my breathing, the only sound aside from the wind that always whipped across these heights. I took the gamble and stood up, leaned over to place the pail below the pump and looked down at my gaunt black face and haunted wild eyes looking back from the depths of the trough. I was no longer the handsome devil Jess had loved. I placed the revolver on the ground and began to work the pump.

I heard movement in the bushes that flanked the woods. I ducked down and picked up the Colt, but there was nothing save an old crow thrashing about looking for food. I knew how he felt as I stood back up and continued to fill the pail. I then placed it next to the trough and crossed the "yard" to a cluster of chokeberry and dogwood bushes and trees that stood along the eastern rim of the ridge adjoining the oak wood. I kept my hand on the Navy Colt in my belt as I approached the shaded grove and the three wooden crosses. One was newer than the other two. I had always intended to replace them with headstones, but had never gotten around to it. But, as Jess had said, its what's in your heart that's the real memorial, not some piece of stone.

"Well daddy, mom, Luke, it's just us again," I took off the blue army hat and held it to my chest. "There's an ill wind coming and I can't say for sure where I'll be when it's blown itself out." I wasn't a praying man so I just stood and thought of them all and wished they were here now in my trials.

I went into the barn to look for any sharp tools, providing they hadn't been stolen. I found an old sickle and a long sharp knife for cutting leather. I went back to the trough, collected the pail, and with the sickle and the knife returned to the cabin.

I closed the door and pulled the bar across and shot the bolts. It had felt good to stretch my legs and get some air. I thought once more about taking off on foot, through the woods and follow the trail up into the mountains. Why not? I could keep moving and they would be hard pressed to keep track of me. But track me they would. It occurred to me that this is what they may assume I'd done and had let me go. What was I thinking? There were some first-class trackers down there and they would lead the mob on regardless of how I wove and ducked and dodged. Only a fool would underestimate the hubris of the chase. I glanced out of the east facing window, imagining Comanche Joe lying still under the roots of some deep oak. He once said he could remain completely still for hours on end, without losing concentration. Well, if he was there, he already knew I was too, so I could safely ignore him unless, of course, he was the one despatched to finish me off. Somehow I never saw that gentle giant as a cold-blooded killer. Nor did I see him as a man to exploit prejudice. He knew as much about intolerance as me.

But human nature had become a foreign land to me. I had not reckoned upon the depths men would plumb to justify lynch mob justice. How does a man read the Holy Book only to draw such perverse conclusions? Perhaps they feared that which they did not understand. Perhaps they are in the service of Satan himself. Perhaps, perhaps.... I had seen how the jaundiced heart spreads its fever like a disease on the wind, until the most just soul is infected. And when the blood is up they move like a herd ...no, not a herd, a pack, scenting the blood of the wounded. And the quarry runs until he can run no more. There he turns and baring his fangs waits for the inevitable.

I feared being caught out in the open. I feared being caught at all. I'd seen what they'd done to men the law could not or would not protect. I'm not a violent man by nature but I had become, like many, hardened to the horrors of watching men die a dozen kinds of agony. It's a sad fact that killing becomes easier the more you do it. It's a shameful act and it makes me wonder at the state of men who see and do too much. Are we fit for society... any of us? I am as blood soaked as the mob.

At Richmond, Captain Stewart ordered us all to keep one round in the chamber for ourselves. He said don't let yourself be taken. There's no telling what they'll do to men like us. He said there was no justice in this war and there won't be much more in peace time. I pulled the Navy Colt from my belt and checked the chambers.

I put the pail of fresh water in the store room and returned and picked up Luke's gun and checked it again. I had one box of twenty shells, which I now opened, beside the sickle and new knife on the refectory table. I was so hungry! I glanced to the window and wondered about going back into the woods to pick more fruit. If they hadn't come before nightfall I would go out but they must be coming soon! "Where are you?" I heard a voice growl. I repeated it. This time I screamed it.

Down in the valley, I could imagine them stoking the latent bloodlust that pulses through the veins of many a man. I could picture them in the gin house making speeches to bring justice to a God-fearing community. The Mayor and the Doc on the bar hollering and not a lawman in sight. Some towns had good respectable lawmen, some wise and some tough, some both. This town seemed unable to maintain any kind of steady hand on the legal tiller. Sure, there was a sheriff but he was a man pinned to a piece of tin for administrative purposes. I never saw a more useless piece of meat than Drummond. Right now he would be in his office sucking on a bottle of whisky to drown out the noise of the howling mob outside his door.

I checked Pa's timepiece and it was past 4 o'clock. They have given me three clear days and they don't know my horse has been stolen, unless the Tunstall boy has told them; in which case they know where I am.

"And, after all you've been through, how can they still want your hide?" Jess had said. I didn't have the words to explain to someone who always saw the best in everyone. But what's done is done and there ain't no way of singing it to a different tune. We'd run so far and so fast ahead of the whispers and the belittlement and the threats. I thought we were home and free but I had underestimated the zeal of good Christians to hunt down their man and for dispensing their unique brand of justice. So we returned to face them. The carpet baggers had moved south bringing Union justice in which I had misplaced my faith. Contempt for the law remained and they took everything. I had nowhere else to go. It seemed right that it should end here, in our home.

I sat back in the rocker and allowed its gentle movement to ease my nerves. I don't know how my heart didn't beat its way out of my chest. At 6 o'clock, I went to the window and retrieved the rifle and shells. I always felt better nursing its more reassuring weight than just the Colt. By 7, my eyelids were drooping as my mind wandered in that half-light between waking and sleep. I was thinking of the Lord and how he sees all things and for all things there is a purpose. I even asked him what good was there in my predicament. What higher purpose was being served? Like the friends of Job, I tested the Lord's patience asking how bad men could escape his justice while good men suffered despite their faith. And Lord, I see myself as a good man. I know that I did things in the war that no man should have to, but I didn't do anything with malice aforethought.

And I don't even know if I killed him. I'd done enough and that was all the reason they needed. It was him or me and he was drunk and I was scared and angry at what he'd done. And the others, well they was egging him on to do what he did, so I don't see how I strayed Lord, unless I should have turned the other cheek like our saviour. In which case I'm too weak and look how my foolish weakness has put so many I love in the ground. After all these weeks and months we just endured and we should have stayed away, but that wasn't enough for a man like me. I needed absolution. I had run out of road. It was only right that I stand and I face whatever's coming up from the valley.

Am I vengeful? In my heart there is a blackness that's spread which demands I take a life for a life. I have become them. It's not what I wanted and neither would Jess who would still, even now, be looking for another way. But I'm not Jess and look where he is now! He was a better man than me and since they took him I will dispense justice the only way I have left. My soul is already damned.

It was getting dark out and my eyelids were heavy. My mind was dull as I tried to remember my own name. I checked Pa's old time piece. It was 8:15. The pots and pans chattered and clanked. They were here.

An Empty Nest

Rhonda Neal

Mr. Ramsden thought quite a lot of himself and took great care of his appearance. Rather like the male birds on his farm, he thought that putting on a good show would attract the attentions of a potential mate. Some birds, he knew steal shiny items to attract females to the nests they build. His approach was not that subtle - he boasted of his wealth and his good prospects. Mainly his courting territory was the local pub, called The Long Boat, where he spouted stories of hidden treasure that was yet to be found. He had proof - sadly just one coin which his recently deceased father had given him - but he was convinced a real hoard was somewhere to be found on the farm.

The barmaid, not much more than eighteen, listened to the tales even when other drinking companions had tired of them. Over the following few weeks, she convinced herself that there must be some truth in them. She did a little research and found there had been several similar finds along the valley. She paid more attention to her story-telling customer and gradually realised his interest in her was more than her ability to pull a good pint of beer. She was impressed by the way he always had plenty of cash in his wallet, as her own purse had always been lacking. She also liked the quality items of jewellery he wore, such as the golden medallion, Rolex watch and gold cufflinks. Her own jewellery was all fake. The farm he owned was large and locally known for being well run and profitable, especially in the days when his father managed it. He enjoyed showing his wealth off. When he asked her out on a date, she accepted and enjoyed all the attention he bestowed on her and she really, really liked the gifts too.

The local people laughed behind their backs when they married, mainly because of the age difference between them, which was in fact over twenty years. He had told her that he was thirty and she told him that she was twenty-five. It did not matter that both knew the other was lying. They each saw something in one another they wanted. Their neighbours said she was a gold digger and he was a silly old fool, but the couple were initially quite happy, she finally having a home of her own and a comfortable life. Mr. Ramsden had the young pretty wife he always wanted and enjoyed being waited on.

Things went along quite well until Mr. Ramsden's true passions surfaced and dominated their lives. His new love was a metal detector and, although encouraged at first by his wife to attempt to find the promised hoard, the hobby soon became an obsession. The farming way of life is hard and, over the years, Mrs. Ramsden took on more responsibilities while her husband spent every spare minute detecting. The prospect of finding the treasure played on both their minds. He wanted to prove he was right to his wife and the local people who scoffed at him. For her, it was always about increasing their wealth and the hope that life could become easier. Instead, things got much harder.

After five years, when yet another flood came and churned up the land, they were virtually stranded in the farmhouse. As the water subsided, the damage to the now failing farm was worse than they expected. They had lost livestock, and many repairs were needed to fences, buildings, and, more urgently, to their rather strained relationship. Instead of tackling these problems, Mr. Ramsden resumed his detecting pursuit. When the Watlington hoard was discovered in Oxfordshire, things took a turn for the worse. Mr. Ramsden thought of nothing else. It became an overwhelming obsession. Meanwhile, Mrs. Ramsden spent more and more time alone, doing more and more of the farm work. Understandably, resentment grew. Most marriages face tests from time to time, infidelity being a common issue, but being cast aside because of a bleeping machine was too much to bear! She started to brood and to fantasize about other lifestyles that did not involve hard work and a neglectful lover. A favourite daydream featured a strong Viking prince, complete with a large sword, amorous intentions and being carried away. Strangely, her husband shared a similar fantasy in which he was the Viking with horned helmet, beard and a full head of thick hair (which he did not possess in real life), and huge chests of treasure. Instead of a sword though, he triumphantly held his trusty metal detector by his side.

One day while Mr. Ramsden was out detecting as usual and Mrs. Ramsden was clearing muddy water from the henhouse, an old admirer came knocking at her door. She was most surprised to see Dennis Fowler, the brewery representative she knew from the pub. She was so glad to see a friendly face that she gave him one of her loveliest smiles and her dark eyes twinkled. He was a well-built man with a mass of longish hair and a thick beard, and she became swept into her fantasy and almost swooned into his strong arms. In fact, Mr. Fowler was certainly no Viking but, like Mrs. Ramsden, certainly had an eye for an opportunity. Her features reminded him of a pretty bird, with her lovely dark eyes and hair of raven black. She made him feel special somehow, and soon he was a regular visitor whenever he was in the area. Mrs. Ramsden regained some of her former energy after re-kindling her love life with her new Viking prince. She made a scarecrow and positioned it so that it could be seen from the road. If the hat was on it indicated to her new admirer that her husband was out detecting (again) and she would welcome a visit. The fact they might be discovered added excitement, especially for Mrs. Ramsden who relished attention.

All was going well until the following Autumn when flooding hit again. The rain started in early November and was relentless. It came in heavy torrents of water, flattening the grass, clogging the soil, filling streams and ditches, and soon bursting the banks of the nearby river. The house and outbuildings remained above the water level, but the worst of it was that Mr. Ramsden was stuck in the house with Mrs. Ramsden. To his credit, he helped move some of the livestock into the cattle barn, but soon abandoned it all again to his wife. He set himself up in the living room, watching old episodes of *Time Team* and drinking whatever alcohol could be found in the house.

When the rain finally stopped in late January, the water subsided more quickly than before, much to Mrs. Ramsden's relief. The damage to the landscape was severe. The stream running along the west side of the old field had changed shape, its edges blurred and silted. When flooding had occurred in the past, the soils had been enriched by the process, so increasing yields, and that always softened the blow. In recent years, the water damage had been far greater. The job to restore the farm was immense and for a time they worked together, but they both knew things were way out of control. Mrs. Ramsden knew there was no time to think of anything else, or anyone else for that matter, as their livelihood was at stake. But soon old habits crept back and Mr. Ramsden became wrapped up in his search for treasure.

By early spring, things on the land had improved and it was then she first noticed the large black bird making regular trips from the old barn to the flattened bank of the stream in the field. It was the flash of something gold that caught her eye and had made her investigate. Making sure Mr. Ramsden was asleep (as usual) on the sofa, she crept out of the house with a torch in hand. The going was slippery and she was cold, as the scruffy overcoat covering her night clothes was insufficient. She crossed the field and made her way down towards the big willow. She shone the beam of light around the base of the tree and was amazed to see golden coins just lying among its roots and the general debris from the flood. There were more coins in the water and the moonlight helped to illuminate them. Forgetting the cold, Mrs. Ramsden grabbed at the coins and jammed them into her pockets. She could feel the fabric of the old coat stretching over her shoulders with the weight. It was a lovely feeling! She filled the pockets of her dressing gown, too. When she had collected all that she could see, she walked slowly back towards the house. Her breathing was ragged with the exertion – gold is heavy after all – but more so from the excitement of finding such a prize, with nothing but a torch! At that moment, she decided that she would keep the gold a secret from her husband. It would be nice to watch him continuing his efforts, knowing that she had beaten him to it. For some time, her loyalty to him had been seeping away like the flood water surrounding the farm.

It was then that she remembered the bird. She made the

small detour to the barn. When inside, she shone the torch around the walls, beams, and rafters. Small areas of the roof had missing tiles and the moonlight broke through. It was the bright eye of the bird, reflecting in the light, which gave away the position of the nest. Although woken from sleep he was fully alert to the unexpected and unwelcome visitor. A ladder was needed to get to the nest, which was now Mrs. Ramsden's objective. She wanted all the treasure for herself - she had earned it.

There were the remains of the old hayloft behind the main 'A' shaped frame of the barn, and the bird was positioned on the horizontal beam close to the eave. The ladder used in the bygone days of the farm was still resting against this frame, but it would be difficult to move. If the ladder would take her weight, she thought she would be able to slide herself along the beam. She took off her old heavy coat and laid it down on an old bale of straw, the gold clinking wonderfully as she did so. Normally, she hated heights, but in the darkness, with the torch tucked down the front of her nighty and the dressing gown belt tied tightly, she started to climb. The gold in the pockets knocked against her legs as she moved. The roof of the barn was in a very poor state, not only because of the holes in the roof, but some large Cotswold stone tiles were hanging precariously above her. She continued her ascent, crawling onto the wide beam and carefully making her way across by shuffling slowly towards the nest. All the while, the crow had been observing her without blinking. This was not the kind of female he had been hoping to attract.

The bird's hoard was considerably less in volume but worth far more in monetary value. There were jewelled gold bracelets, brooches and a couple of pendant necklaces hanging over the side of the rough twigs, strewn like Christmas decorations. Just as she stretched her hand forward, the loose tile above slipped a little and she let out a small gasp. Her additional weight on the old woodwork had triggered some structural changes. Next thing she knew, several tiles came crashing to the ground, hitting an old oil drum and the noise echoed loudly. Mrs. Ramsden then heard the kitchen door slam, so she switched off the torch. Just as her torch light went out, another beam appeared, as the large door of the barn opened and her husband's voice boomed out: "Who's there? I've got a gun!"

Mrs. Ramsden shivered as cold sweat trickled down her face. She did not want to be found, so with extra adrenaline coursing through her body, she pulled herself further under the eave at the edge of the old hayloft. Her husband was a good shot and easily excited. She decided to wait things out quietly, as she did not want to explain herself. The bird had also chosen to be quiet, not wanting to give its location away. The flashlight circled the barn, and when the tiles were found on the drum and ground. Mr. Ramsden looked up momentarily, cursed, and headed back to the sofa and to

Tony Robinson (the presenter of *Time Team*) which had been put on pause. When the door to the house slammed shut and the television restarted, Mrs. Ramsden allowed herself to breathe normally. She knew she would not be missed. The jewellery was now much closer and within reach, so she took her chance. The bird crowed this time and lunged forward to peck her hand. This made her jump so much that she hit her head very hard on the rafter. Everything went dizzy and she fell forward, unconscious. All went quiet, and while the bird did not like the proximity of his new neighbour, he settled warily to sleep again.

Mr. Ramsden was a little put out that there was not a cup of tea close to hand when he awoke. He focussed on the clock on the mantelpiece, and saw it was already seven fifteen. The house was very quiet, no radio playing, no fire in the grate and, rather disturbingly, no smell of frying bacon. He called his wife's name several times. He decided to check the bedroom and found the bed made. After an hour or so of looking around the house and buildings, he had still found no trace of her. The metal detector stood in the hallway waiting patiently for him, so he decided that she must have gone out early and forgotten to leave a message.

When he had convinced himself of this scenario, he took his detector and headphones and went out towards the bottom field, which ran parallel to the road. This field was closest to the river and had flooded badly. He was not sure why he wanted to work there this morning, but he had a feeling it might be worth it. He decided to start by the wall of the old barn, under the trees with the crow's nests. Working away beneath the trees, the crows were disturbed and sent loud craws so he gradually worked on further out into the field.

Several metres away, the old scarecrow was crumpled and slumped forward. Mr. Ramsden realized it was dressed in his old clothes. In fact, it looked remarkably like him. For a moment, he remembered his wife and gave a wry smile at her sense of humour. As he got nearer to it, he could see that the pole, which his clone was tied to, had sunk deeply into the ground after the flood and had probably not been moved since then. Out of some remnant of affection for his wife, he decided to re-position it for her and, as he did so, felt a slight tightening in his chest. He straightened the figure up, pushed it into shape, and found the old hat wedged in the pocket so put it on the scarecrow's bald head. He stood it up and pushed the pole back into the ground. He smiled at the similarity and thought she might be pleased to see he had taken interest in her efforts.

The soil near to the pole was full of wet silt. Purely on a whim, he decided to pass the detector over the area and was stupefied when a strong signal indicated there was something metallic. Thinking it must be something to do with the scarecrow, he started to dig. After a couple of spades of earth were removed, water filled the spaces. So he dug again a little faster and the water continued to fill the void. Soon it became a race between removal of the soil and the water replacing the space made.

After several minutes of more frantic digging, he thought he saw something silvery at the bottom of the hole. He quickly thrust his hand into the silty water and felt around. Nothing. So, he recommenced digging, his heart and imagination racing at the prospect of his dreams coming true. Again, the silvery object appeared in its muddy pool. Again, he thrust his hand in and groped about until he felt the edge of a slim, flat object. "It's the hoard, my hoard!" he shouted out loud. He pulled at the object, gasping and now crying. For the second time, he thought of his wife and felt that pang in his chest again. The sensation started to intensify to real pain that radiated over his shoulder and down his arm. He had felt something similar before, but not as bad as this. Even when he knew he was dying, his last thought was of his two great loves, and he realized he would never see them again. He collapsed forward into the hole and came to rest, still clutching his metal detector - the scarecrow the only witness to his passing.

From her hayloft nest, Mrs. Ramsden had been unconscious until the sound of her husband's voice in the distance had roused her. She managed to look out of the hole in the roof to witness him digging and she thought she would have time to get home without being discovered.

Then it struck her that he must have realised she was missing and clearly thought more of pursuing his ridiculous hobby than of coming to her rescue! She was rather muddled, felt pain at the back of her head and was nauseous. She looked at the crow, still sitting in its nest, and noticed his decorous jewellery. Thinking quickly, she tossed one of the coins along the beam and, to her amazement, the bird took the bait. So she helped herself to his valuables, while he retrieved the coin. She very carefully moved across the beam, concentrating on the ladder, and returned safely to the ground. Once there, she staggered slightly as she walked towards the house. Her thoughts were focussed on getting herself up to bed.

Waking late in the afternoon to the sound of a familiar engine, she sat upright slowly and painfully and noticed the blood on her pillow. Feeling the wound at the back of her head, she slowly stood up and went to the window. Dennis was just getting out of the car. By the time she had got down the stairs, her senses were returning.

As she opened the door, she could see the concern appear on his face. He helped her into the kitchen and she sat heavily in a chair at the kitchen table. She told him what she could remember, but it was rather confused. He knew in any crisis situation the most important thing was to make tea. While filling the kettle, he looked out of the window and noticed a crow fly over the field down towards the river bank and disappear behind the old willow. Not really knowing what to say, he mentioned something about the activities of crows. She turned towards the window, with a sudden flash of the night's events passing through her mind. She asked Dennis why he had come and he explained that the scarecrow had his hat on. Checking the time, for now it was late afternoon, she realised that her husband had not been in the house all the while she had been sleeping upstairs.

They both headed outside. It was raining again as they walked towards the field where Mrs. Ramsden had seen her husband working earlier that morning. They found his body in the shallow pool with his hand clasped around the pole of the metal detector. He was dead.

Dennis took charge, helping her back into the house and lying her down on the sofa. Both of them were genuinely shocked. The ambulance arrived sometime later, together with the police. When the paramedics had tended her wound, the police wanted to clarify the events. Mrs. Ramsden was mostly truthful, explaining she had heard a noise in the barn, went to investigate, and had hit her head. When she woke made her way back to the house and to bed. Both she and Dennis did not mention the role of the scarecrow in the matter, saying he called in simply by chance. The police seemed satisfied with her account and left her to rest.

When everyone had gone, she went up to her room and sat on the bed. She felt rather shocked but became rather excited when she noticed the torch poking out of her dressing gown pocket. She checked to see if the contents of the pockets were still there, and, in her rush, many coins fell onto the carpet. Remembering her old coat, she went to the barn to collect it. Glancing up, she noticed that the bird's nest was empty and unadorned.

A few weeks later, following the inquest result of 'Death by Natural Causes', she returned to the farm for the last time. Her bags were already packed, but she had two more jobs to do before leaving. Firstly, she went to the field where her husband had died and gently laid the scarecrow down, removing his hat and putting it firmly in his pocket. She smiled wryly and enjoyed kicking the metal detector which rather absurdly still had a weak flashing light pulsating. She walked across the old field, the day being warm and sunny, and the crows as usual were flying noisily about. Then she heard the taxi arriving so she stopped by the willow and looked around. She quickly slid her wedding ring off her finger and placed it at the base of the tree, where she hoped it would be found by a certain black bird that liked such things, and skipped back towards the house.

A Second Chance

Lucy McGregor

The tattered billboard was barely legible under the vicious scrawl of graffiti, outrage and anger spewing violent and crude obscenities. The lashing rain was loosening the paint, trickling colour like trails of blood down the boarded up shopfront below and drawing the eye to the flash of the crime scene warning holotape.

Huddled in the shelter of the news stand opposite, Rachel hunched deeper into her dark coat and scanned her surroundings. Peeling paintwork, litter in the gutter, little shops with darkened windows... a dirty old street squashed into the shadows by the relentless rise of the skytowers. Some of the stained concrete buildings were derelict; others were occupied with cheap electronics stores, net booths, massage parlours; optimistic start-ups next to struggling family businesses that hadn't managed to keep up with the times next to outright criminal enterprises. Half the properties on this street could use a raid by MetForce.

Today the foul weather was doing its job, sweeping the

area clear of anyone who might want to make trouble. Even the news vendor was an auto, lights blinking slowly as it waited for activation. In fact, there was just one person in sight, a slim androgynous figure picking a fastidious path across the sodden pavement. Rachel noted critically the half-shaven head, the green-dyed hair, the slim garment seemingly composed of buckles and straps and strategically placed cut-outs, and the glitter of wires.

"Do you really think that's appropriate to wear to work, Cam?"

Heavily made-up eyes glared. "It is when you get called in half way through your night off. Just so you know, I was paying deep attention to a faux-intellectual theory about spiritual growth induced through ecstasy."

"Blonde?"

"And stacked out to here. You're signing the overtime for this, right?"

"I am if you earn it."

Cam groaned. "And for this I gave up my personal demonstration! You're a cruel woman. All right. What can't wait?"

She nodded at the abandoned pet shop. "We're going in there."

Cam looked over at it sceptically. "You know it's been searched, right?"

"They missed something."

"Oh, sure. The crime of the century, and our best and

brightest just skipped over all the evidence and left it lying around here for a couple of grunts on their day off to swing by and pick up."

"It's got to be somewhere."

"Destroyed. Lost. Or hidden in one of his other properties, where the team that are actually assigned to this case are actually searching right now. He's been arrested, boss, what are we doing here?"

"You know he's claiming that it was all just a terrible mistake?" Rachel rounded on her partner. "That, what with the communication issues, he had no idea what they were? That's bullshit! He knew. Everything he did to cover up their origin planet and stop anyone from investigating them... Commercial sensitivity? Please. He couldn't let anyone see what... see who his 'pets' really were. Well, somewhere in there is the evidence that will prove it."

"And you think you're going to find it? When no one in the whole Force has been able to nail it to him?"

"The focus has all been on that horror show up at the Peaks. All the details of the operation were kept up there. But he didn't move there until after he'd started coining it in and could afford the new premises. If we want to know what he knew at the start – this is the place." She led the way across the street and flicked the nail of her little finger against the holographic MetForce seal over the lock. The light wavered, then flared bright and went out, accepting her identification. "Don't worry. I don't expect to find anything alone. That's why I invited the best tech in the Force to join me."

"Oh, really?" Cam grumbled. "When are you expecting them, then? Can I go home?"

"Cute. No one likes – ugh." The stench rolled out as the door swung open, stuffy air thick with guano and decay. Rachel blanched; Cam's skin was already bleached unnaturally pale as a matter of fashion, but the technician pulled back, nose wrinkling in disgust.

"Guess no one cleaned out the cages. Hope they found homes for the animals at least."

They entered cautiously, dust stirring round their feet as the lights flickered into life. The cheap strip lights were sickly yellow, grudgingly lightening the gloom. The shop bore the signs of a Force raid; the window had been smashed and a rack of shelves against it collapsed, glass, splinters and sawdust scattered across the floor. Further back the room was clearer, shelves stacked with dusty bags and boxes of pet food, toys, accessories, and a section full of now-empty tanks and cages. No graffiti in here; the poster filling the wall behind the counter had dirt splashed across it but was clear enough. It featured an image that had dominated the holonet recently; a white four-legged creature with ring after ring of delicate frills puffed out down the length of it so that the general impression was a sleek body floating in a cloud of fronds. It was facing the camera, and Rachel, looking into its honey-coloured eyes, was unable, now, to see them as anything but full of fear, confusion, and pain.

In the background of the poster a man was standing; a tall, thin man, balding, with square-rimmed glasses; a man who looked entirely inoffensive, but whose confident smile seemed now wolfish. Rachel narrowed her eyes.

"Ew." Behind her, Cam was hesitating in the doorway, looking with clear unhappiness at the filthy room. Rachel took pity. "You do behind the counter; I'll do the shop proper?"

"Works for me!" Cam picked a way past the worst of the mess. "Hey, boss? It's not like you to mess with someone else's case. This seems kind of… personal."

Pulling on her sterile gloves, Rachel paused. Eventually she said, "Tally really wanted to have one of these guys for a pet. This school friend of hers had one."

"Yeah? They cost a bomb though, didn't they?"

"Her dad offered to buy it for her."

Cam snorted. "Divorce guilt? What did you say?"

Rachel half-smiled. "Oh, the usual fight. I said it was all right for him out there on the asteroid earning that obscene wage and making out like it's so hard on him. Like I couldn't see some woman's silk dressing gown draped on a chair in the background. Anyway, I lost it and told him that it was all very well for him to spoil Tally and be the one who produces expensive presents and never enforces vegetables and homework, but when it came to pets who would it be that had to feed it and clean it out and look after it, and I wasn't having any of it."

"Okay, so?"

"So, I was this close to giving a sentient creature – a person – to my daughter as a pet." She winced. "And it's not like I had a good reason to refuse. Just pettiness. What if I'd decided to be a bigger person that day?"

Cam shuddered. "Ugh. Okay. I get it. Still… it wouldn't have been your fault. You didn't know."

"That's the point. There's thousands of families out there right now who perpetrated that horror, and they didn't know. But this guy?" She stabbed a finger at the man in the poster. "He knew."

"Does it matter? Ignorance is no defence, as they say. There's no disputing the facts of what he did. He'll get what's coming whether or not the judge believes his story."

Rachel started lifting cages down from the shelves on the walls, quickly checking through the contents of each, and stacking them on the floor. "Yes. It matters. Tally and her friends and their families, they're innocent dupes. This guy and his people? Pure evil. I need to prove that. I need everyone to know that. Now what's this?"

Cam looked up from distastefully pulling open drawers with minimal disgusted fingertip contact. "Got something?"

"Maybe." Rachel dragged a penlight out of her pocket and turned it full beam into the back corner of the shelving unit. "Something a bit odd with the construction here."

"Ooh, is it a secret door?" Cam drawled, eyebrows rising.

"Haven't I told you no one likes a funny cop? This support's thicker than the others. Could be a hollow section behind. Got some pliers or tweezers or something?"

A multi-tool appeared in the corner of her vision, and she reached for it absently, then almost dropped it and looked down in surprise. The tool looked wicked, slick black and heavy in the hand, with glimmering diamond edges. "Cam, who carries around something like this? Is this even legal?"

"Do you want it or not? It's okay, it's for work."

"I want it." She folded out the pliers and turned back to the suspicious unit. "And when we get back to the station you can submit a report explaining why you have it on you when you were on your day off and not prepared for work at all."

"Harsh, boss!"

Rachel ignored the comment. There was a hollow compartment, after all; and with the pliers she could reach into it. There was something in there that moved as the tip of the tool touched it. She altered her grip to open the pliers slightly and fished carefully after whatever it was.

"Got it!"

"You realise it'll be some piece of rubbish that just fell behind the shelves and got forgotten, right?"

Rachel held her breath as she carefully eased the little lump out of its hiding place, then spat and rubbed dust off with her thumb. "You miss your guess, Cam."

"A data core? Wow, living in the past much?"

"I would say don't be a tech snob, but I know that's a lost cause. Lots of people still use solid data storage." She shrugged and gestured around. "Especially the kind of small business that can't afford to fully update their set up every time a new kind of tech comes out."

"To the lab, then? You want to keep looking around here for a bit?"

"Really? You didn't believe we were going to find anything and now that we actually have you don't even want to look?"

"Uh uh." Cam lifted an admonishing finger. "I am not plugging that thing in. Look at the state of this place. I bet that thing is corrupted enough to scramble my wires into next week."

"Even I know that a dirty environment doesn't actually induce data corruption."

"And any self-respecting criminal would have stuffed it with malware."

"Cam, the only reason you don't have a PhD in interactive implant firewall tech is because you got bored as it was too easy! Your implant is the safest on the planet, or probably in the whole galaxy for that matter."

Cam pulled a face and gingerly picked up the squat little object. "It's funny how your faith in me doesn't make me feel any better. If this thing spikes me, you're going to be working alone for at least a week while I get scrubbed, you know."

"I will even sign your on-duty hazard payout."

"You'd better." Cam flipped the data stick over. "It's got a standard jack, at least. All right, here goes." A fine golden wire was already snaking out from beneath the buckle at the wrist of the technician's shirt. The tip of the wire lifted into the air, hesitated for an instant, then darted forwards and plunged into the data stick socket.

Rachel watched wires illuminate under the skin of Cam's shaven head, tracing an eerie net across the technician's skull. She was neither disgusted nor alarmed; she knew perfectly well that the working part of Cam's implant was a tiny, invisible chip at the back of the neck; all the rest was purely an aesthetic choice.

After a moment Cam's eyes opened, slightly unfocused. "That was anti-climactic."

"You're in?"

"Yeah, no security here at all. Just a load of data files. Looks like planetary survey records. Hang on." The technician frowned. "Cheap ones. Looks like he ordered a whole raft of them. Probably speculatively. Must have realised that if he found a new species of alien pet he'd be made."

"Big risk. Even if you use some cut price automated probe outfit it's not cheap to scan an unexplored system."

Cam shrugged. "People buy lottery tickets. Okay, so he's gambling. He needs to find a species that's new, that can survive in earth-type conditions, and preferably that's cute. So when his results came back with –"

"He must have thought he was the luckiest man alive." Rachel said, grimly. "Have you got the right record?"

"Searching… ah." Cam's hairless brows lifted. "Yes, I actually have. Is there a screen somewhere here? There's video."

"I've got a port." Rachel retrieved the flimsy roll screen from her coat pocket and flicked it at the wall, where it unrolled and clung, shimmering slightly, against the stained paintwork.

"Okay, casting what I'm seeing over."

There was a blur of motes, and then the video resolved itself onto the portable screen. Rachel looked at it hungrily. Very poor quality, compressed to save size – the probe that picked it up would have had the smallest possible lightcaster, not enough to kick a larger data packet past the limitations of conventional travel through the intervening space. It was date stamped, time stamped – the lab would have to check that out, establish that was original, but they had no reason to think otherwise – and the date was what she needed to fix. And the contents –

"Would you look at that?" said Cam, softly. The technician leaned forwards, examining text and little graphs spread across the lower edge of the screen. "Microwaves. Radio waves… Boss, they're pumping this stuff out into their atmosphere like we did a few generations ago. I think they have satellites."

"Cam…"

"And I think they don't have… I'm not seeing lightcaster bloom here. But they're high tech. Do you understand how unlikely this is? Carbon based biology, oxygen breathers, even a roughly equivalent tech level… this is the most similar alien species we've ever encountered. The kind of similar we thought we might never find."

"Cam… look at the video."

Rachel already had her eyes on the main screen. The camera was sweeping across a landscape of graceful sweeping structures of striated rock, brilliant bands of brown and grey running clear through; and at first she thought of it as mountainous, until she started to realise that the clean organised lines of it and the regular openings weren't quite natural. The sky, glimpsed between the tall peaks was vivid blue, so bright that the colour quality of the cheap cast couldn't do it justice and bleached out. All around was a bustle of movement, the little white creatures that she still had to remind herself to think of as people, hurrying in all directions in bright flurries of cloud-like fronds and as she watched her eyes resolved the motion into organised travel, and she realised –

"It's a city," breathed Cam, beside her. "Look, the main street has the most traffic, and there's people going in and out of that structure over there – must be important."

"Station."

"Could be! Transport hub. They must have powered transport. I wonder what it is?"

"It's beautiful." Rachel said, softly.

"This is a game changer, boss. I mean, at a civilizational level. This could be... what we've got, right here, this is history. This is when we see the future change – forever."

"Assuming that the worst possible examples of humanity don't mean that what we actually get are years of war."

Cam looked up at her, quickly. "We've caught him, boss."

"If we can't prove that he's guilty – that he deliberately deceived us – then we're all equally culpable. All complicit." She shrugged. "No one wants to admit they're the bad guys. If people start getting defensive over it, start insisting that we did nothing wrong – if politicians climb on the bandwagon of that stance? And their government, whatever structure they have, condemns that – calls us, I don't know, holocaust deniers, and refuses to let it go?"

Cam was silent. Rachel watched shadow and lights shifting under the technician's translucent skin.

After a moment the screen quietly dimmed, rippling into shadows and then dullness, and Cam held out the data-stick. "Well. Here's your proof." The connecting wire jerked free and slithered away. "I copied everything. So we have a record. Just in case."

"Thanks."

Cam nodded, locks of green hair brushing against one

earlobe. "Are you heading back in, then?"

Rachel nodded. "You weren't wrong. This has to go to the lab, get verified…"

"Yeah. Let's go."

"You don't have to come for the paperwork. I know it's your day off. You can get back to the theory of ecstasy, if you like."

"And I'm going to let this go, after coming this far?" Cam turned on a heel in the doorway, a slim and fantastic figure, and flashed a sudden smile. "You're such a cynic, boss. You need to have more faith in people."

As Rachel followed her partner out, the neon scrolling headlines above the news stand opposite were brilliant through the rain.

ALIEN LANGUAGE CRACKED – COMMUNICATION WITH SISTER SPECIES FINALLY POSSIBLE – "NO EXCUSE FOR SUFFERING" SAYS FIRST MINISTER – SUPPORT PLEDGED TO REPATRIATE VICTIMS – MINISTER PROMISES: "HUMANITY WILL WORK TO DESERVE A SECOND CHANCE."

A Team Player

Jackie Vickers

The Glossops came to live next door soon after Douglas Glossop retired. They were a quiet self-contained couple with little to say. We asked them round for drinks and to meet the neighbours, but they would only take fruit juice and seemed ill-at-ease.

"They look like salt and pepper pots," John said afterwards, for they were both small and plump and stood very stiffly.

We had spent much of the summer visiting family and friends and it was not until September that I finally got to lift my trombone case down from the top of the wardrobe and blow off the dust. There had been no time to practice and I hurried out to rehearsal feeling harassed and ill-prepared. Douglas Glossop was gardening and saw me struggling to find room for the trombone in the small boot of my car.

"Is that yours?" His eyes gleamed behind his glasses.

"I don't play very well, but it's great for relieving tension." I smiled at him, closed the boot and settled myself in the driver's seat. Douglas had followed me around and now hung onto the door handle.

"Band practice?"

"Our local Orchestral Society," I said, and started the

engine.

He nodded and smiled and disappeared behind the hedge. The next evening Douglas knocked on our door.

"Have you room for any more cellos?" he asked, rocking up and down on the balls of his feet. "I used to play in our local orchestra, where we lived before. In our last season we played the Elgar Cello Concerto," he looked down at his shiny shoes, "with a guest soloist, of course." He was quite breathless, whether from excitement or because he was unused to speaking so much, was hard to say. "I know some orchestras have auditions, but perhaps a recommendation from my conductor would... ." He tailed off, looking anxious.

Our organisation was at times chaotic, but everyone was committed and no-one liked the formality of auditions. We preferred not to judge each other and relied on our weaker players to practice harder or drop out if they could not keep up. We were short of cellists, so Douglas was told he would be welcome. We rehearsed in an old church hall, notable for its stale smell of neglect. It had high exposed roof timbers but the acoustics were rather good, though some said the only thing to recommend it was the quality of the real ales sold at the pub opposite. On the whole, we were a happy crowd and the only major episode of disagreement in years had been the choice of music. The traditionalists among us wanted nothing written after Elgar while the progressives insisted on more modern pieces. There were some, mainly comprising our leader and most of the first violins, who declared they would do anything short of blackmail to get late twentieth-century pieces included on the programme.

"At least let us play some through. You may be pleasantly surprised," pleaded the bassoonist who had a particular attachment to Shostakovich.

But our treasurer would not entertain it. "Are you aware of the cost of hiring a complete set of parts for, say, one of his symphonies? And what if most of us do not like it?"

"Worse still," said the percussionist, "What if we couldn't play it!"

Fortunately, our conductor pointed out that our likes and dislikes were immaterial. "If the audience doesn't like it we may well cease to exist. Music lovers in this town are very supportive and enthusiastic, but who knows how they might respond if compelled to sit through anything too challenging. Many years ago, before most of you had joined, we had played some Benjamin Britten, something adapted for orchestra from *Peter Grimes*. It was very coolly received. In fact, we were more or less warned off trying anything like that again." He shuddered at the memory.

"Shostakovich can hardly be seen as challenging" grumbled the bassoonist, but he let the matter drop.

Douglas came to rehearsal the following week and joined a group of us afterwards, at *The King's Head*. In the tradition of most amateur societies, we were arguing, in our usual noisy way, over whether or not we needed a rota for putting up stands and clearing up afterwards.

Douglas looked bemused as voices were raised, elbows jostled and little pools of beer appeared on the table. "I enjoyed that slow movement," he said to no-one in particular, "I always feel Brahms is especially moving."

There was an embarrassed silence, then one of the horn players turned towards him and smiled, "Brahms is a new departure for us."

Douglas nodded and looked down at his fruit juice. The conversation never quite got going after that and he never came back to *The King's Head*.

"He only seems to talk about music," I said to John later that night.

"Odd fellow, but harmless I suppose," he shrugged, turning back to the football.

The following week we started on Beethoven's Fifth. All his orchestral works go down well at our concerts and we had already played the first four symphonies with some success. This week, though, our conductor seemed to be having problems. There were several dissonances from near the front which sounded as though a string player was having trouble with his intonation. Then Douglas must have miscounted at the end of the coda, for a single deep chord vibrated in that breathless silence that follows one of Beethoven's dramatic finales. All eyes were on Douglas who sat, motionless, looking fixedly at his music. After a long pause, Bill put his baton down on his music stand.

"Only six weeks to the concert," he said with a stiff smile.

Afterwards Douglas scuttled away, speaking to no-one.

"Can't you have a word with him, Henry?" Bill was walking up and down, twiddling his baton. "As leader of the cellos, you know."

Henry zipped up his canvas cello case and straightened up. "I can't teach the man to count at his age. Either he can or he can't."

Bridget, my fellow trombonist, snapped her case shut and started folding up the stand. She was one of the few players always ready to wade into a debate for the sake of her principles.

"I'm tired of Bill carrying on as though we were the Berlin Philharmonic. Maybe someone will mess up during the concert. Maybe Douglas, maybe someone else. So what? We came together to make music and people make mistakes. We're amateurs, end of story."

I shrugged my shoulders. "Tell Bill then. I'm past caring."

She rounded on me. "Every one of us should care, or that poor man will be a scapegoat for all our mistakes." She turned away and marched off to find Bill. She was a large woman and her long skirt caught at stands and cases as she forced her way to the front. As I left the hall I heard her loudly condemning Bill for his intolerance.

The concert went well, despite the many mishaps during rehearsals. Nevertheless, Bill said his nerves wouldn't stand another season and something had to be done before the summer.

He proposed auditions. "Though there may be more than a few of us who are not quite up to it," he said with a sly smile.

"Unworkable," snorted Bridget. "Who will sit in judgement on us? And we might lose half the orchestra."

"After all," I said, hoping to mollify her, "we're not after perfection. That's not the point."

"Indeed," she said, allowing the mix of condensation and spit to run out of her instrument onto the side of my shoe.

In the end, the auditions idea was dropped and we muddled along through the winter months and into spring.

One warm weekend in May, Joyce Glossop looked over the fence and proposed a musical evening.

"What?" said John, when he came in, hot and sweaty from mowing the lawn.

"Just me, I think," I said. "Douglas must have found some music for cello and trombone!"

The Glossops had made it into something of an occasion. Douglas wore a suit, and plates and cake-forks were set out on an embroidered cloth. They said they were sorry I had not brought John as they had heard he was a musician.

"He plays the accordion very well and he belongs to a folk group," I said, amused to see how Douglas drew back.

"You mean like Morris Men?" he said, looking bewildered.

I had misjudged the formality of the occasion and felt ill-at-ease in my jeans and cotton shirt. They insisted I played first, then Douglas followed with Joyce accompanying him on the piano. His cello part was straightforward but the accompaniment required an accomplished pianist.

"I didn't know you played," I said, impressed.

"Only with Douglas," she flushed and looked away.

"Will you play something else?" I asked her as she tidied away her music and left the piano.

Douglas frowned. "I thought it would be a good idea to hear the experts." He held up a CD. "My latest acquisition. Unaccompanied cello sonatas."

I looked at Joyce, but she was staring out at the garden. Her hands lay on her lap, moving constantly as she turned her wedding ring round and round. I wondered how such a hesitant and anxious individual like Douglas could dominate his wife when she was so much the better musician. He bobbed about the room fetching music and CDs and adjusting his music stand, his wife's gaze never leaving him. And then I realised she was trying to spare him embarrassment. He didn't seem to have any insight but was being ably protected from the results of his own mediocrity by a watchful Joyce.

Later that month our orchestra hit a rocky patch and every Thursday night brought another clutch of minor disasters. Our bassoonist broke two front teeth in a cycling accident and the better of the two cornet players was transferred to his firm's office in Rome. And Douglas was still making mistakes, some more noticeable than others. Bill continued to urge Henry to tutor him in some way and Henry continued to resist the idea.

There were now only a few rehearsals left before our summer concert.

"I wish we could get rid of him," groaned Bill, his head in his hands at the bar of *The King's Head*. He turned as I approached.

"I'd like a word," he whispered, "Let me get you a drink."

I thought this must be something momentous as Bill was famous for dodging his round. He led me to a table well away from our crowd.

"You live next door to the Glossops, don't you?"

"Yes," I said warily.

"I was wondering," he cleared his throat," could you have a word with his wife?"

"What about?"

Bill picked up his glass, sighed, then put it down again. "It's not a bad little orchestra. We have our strengths and weaknesses and it has been a pleasure, and hard work too, but a real pleasure..." he tailed off.

"Joyce Glossop," I prompted, but he seemed not to hear.

"It's a very exposed position, you know, standing up there in front of everyone. You become the public face of the orchestra. People stop me in the street and say nice things about our concerts," he sighed again. "It won't be so obvious to you, at the back with the brass. But for the strings, you know, you can feel the tension. It's like a collective holding of breath as they wonder when he'll drop the next brick, so to speak."

"He's very keen," I said, thinking of Douglas hovering by the hedge. "Nearly Thursday," he would say. Last week, he was stuttering with excitement for he had heard rumours of a Mozart overture for next season. Had I heard? Could it be *The Magic Flute?*

"You have to be more than keen," Bill said, "you have to play in tune. Do you suppose he has other hobbies? I wonder if you could sound out his wife. Maybe suggest a different activity. Doesn't the Dramatic Society meet on Thursdays?"

"Douglas is very shy," I reminded him.

"Well, bowls or something. See what you can do."

"I can't see how I can approach Joyce," I said to John, hoping he might come up with something.

"It's Bill's responsibility," he said. "Nothing to do with

you. He just can't face telling Douglas he's no good."

"It's not that he's a bad player," I objected, "It's just his counting. And he's so keen."

John shrugged. "Either way, it's not your problem."

The following Saturday morning, I met Joyce coming out of the post-office.

"Your laburnum is magnificent," I said. "It lights up the whole road."

She seemed not to hear, but touched my arm. "I'm worried about Douglas." Joyce looked harassed. "It's the concert. Douglas spends so much time practising and looks quite worn out. I tell him no-one expects perfection from amateurs, but he gets annoyed and says "an orchestra is a team and we are all team players." He has high blood pressure, you know."

A week later, a siren and a flashing blue light had us both at the window. We saw Joyce clutching a large bag, following the stretcher into the ambulance. It sped off noisily into the night.

Douglas had suffered a slight stroke, Joyce told me the next day. "With medication and rest, they say, he should recover completely. . . eventually."

I wondered how Douglas would react to prolonged rest. I saw him lying in bed, listening to his cello sonatas, his fingers moving along imaginary strings. I took a pot plant around.

"He's sleeping," she said.

She looked in control again, there was a smell of baking and her hair was back to its tightly curled style.

"He listens to a lot of music. With headphones, of course," she added with a small smile.

"Providential!" cried Bill when I told him.

"That's unkind."

"Oh. You know what I mean," he said. "We'll send him flowers from 'The Orchestra'."

"It's not a proper stroke, as I understand it. He doesn't have any paralysis. It's more of a warning." But Bill was no longer listening.

"I don't suppose he'll be coming back - ever," he muttered to himself, with a foolish smile.

"The poor man will be so disappointed to miss the concert," said Bridget.

The dress rehearsal had gone particularly well. It was the usual mix of apprehension and excitement, and the first time in nearly a year that people were chatting, laughing and joking.

Bill chivvied them, "There still needs to be some tension to get the best from a performance," he said, as he went to open the heavy mahogany door for someone struggling with their instrument.

It was Douglas, red-faced with exertion. He trotted across to his seat and put his cello down.

"I knew you'd be glad to see me," he said, his eyes blinking rapidly as he looked around at the silent crowd. "I just couldn't let you down."

Outlaw's Trail to Nowhere

Martin Marais

ZERO

The horseman drew his mount to a halt. He watched an old man step from the shadows of the canopied veranda of his house.

"Howdy," the old man said.

The horseman thought he saw a look of recognition in the bright blue eyes of the old man. He leaned forward and scrutinised his ragged old face.

"Do I know you?" he asked.

The old man looked at him for a moment, as though searching for something. "I don't believe so," he replied. There seemed to be an edge of resignation in his voice.

The horseman furrowed his brow. Crazy old coot, he thought, either I know him or I don't, there's no half way house with that sort of thing.

"But I know you," the old man continued gaily.

The horseman was suddenly tense. He dropped his hand to the well-oiled Colt that hung on his right hip. He scanned the neat vegetable gardens and ran his eye over the stand of maize set back from the house. But he saw no-one hiding in the long early-evening shadows. His eyes shifted back to the old man.

"I know you're a Texas Ranger," the old man grinned.

His otherwise perfect, white teeth were punctuated with regular gaps that gave him a comical countenance.

The man on the horse relaxed and lifted his hand to touch the shiny metal star pinned to his chest. He smiled to himself. *Of course he knows that, anyone would.*

"You're after someone."

The Ranger wasn't sure if this was a question or a statement. If it was a question, the answer was obvious, what other reason would a Texas Ranger have for being out here, so far from civilisation? Only a mad man would build a house in this god-forsaken place. He was not inclined to answer the old fool, but, in the end, he had no need to, for the old man continued to babble on.

"And …," he paused and rubbed his chin as a mischievous smile played across his lined features, "I reckon, your name is Seb."

The Ranger's eyebrows shot up. He narrowed his eyes at the old man.

"How do you know that?"

The old man shrugged gleefully.

"Just a wild guess. You look like a Seb. You look like someone I know who goes by that name. My name's Robert, Robert McGregor."

The old man hesitated, as though waiting for something to happen – when it did not, he continued, "Come, come on inside."

"I need to press on," said the Ranger. "Like you said, I'm

on the trail of someone."

The old man looked at the sky behind the Ranger. The first stars were just visible in the darkening heavens.

"You're going to have to set up camp soon. You might as well stay here for the night, as spend it out in the open. I have a comfortable bed you could use. I have two beds, so you won't even have to share."

The offer was very tempting. The Ranger could not remember the last time he had slept in a bed.

"And I'm a good cook," the old man added. "Beans, eggs, corn on the cob and corned beef. And as much coffee as you can drink."

Hmm, thought the Ranger, he did like corned beef.

"Thank you, Mister, I will take you up on your offer."

"Robert," the old man reminded him.

"Sure, Robert," the Ranger said as he dismounted stiffly. "Where shall I stable my horse, Robert?"

"Just go to the end of the house," the old man pointed, "You'll find it. Everything you need'll be there."

"Thank you."

The Ranger led his horse along the length of the house. He found the stable easily enough and went in. A lantern lit the interior. It was in immaculate condition. In one stall a donkey ate fresh straw. The Ranger led his horse into the other. The hungry animal immediately started to munch on the bundle of hay that hung on the wall at the end of the enclosure. The Ranger removed his saddle and kit, and slung it over the partition. He found a brush and gave the animal a thorough rub down, brushing days' worth of dust from its hide. He checked its hooves and shoes and ran an expert hand over its withers and legs. It was in fine fettle, a little on the skinny side, perhaps, but, generally, in very good condition. He was pleased. He liked to think that being good at horsemanship was one of his favourable points, and the Lord knew he did not have many of those. He gathered his gear, extinguished the lantern and gave his horse a friendly pat. She rumbled amiably at him. He walked from the darkness of the stable into the growing gloom of the approaching night. He tramped along the veranda and entered the house. Standing in the doorway for a moment he scanned the tidy kitchen. The old man has too much time on his hands, the Ranger concluded. Then he licked his lips as a mouth-watering aroma of cooking wafted over him.

"Come in, come in, sit down," the old man gesticulated not looking up from his cooking.

The Ranger dropped his kit by the door, stepped across the slate-floored kitchen and took a seat at the table. It was set for two people. He lifted the jug, poured himself a glass of water and took a long draft. It was deliciously cold and tasted sweet and clean.

"That's beautiful water," he commented.

"I have a deep well out back," the old man relied absently. "I must remember to replenish your water bag, before you leave tomorrow."

"I'll remind you," said the Ranger grinning to himself, thinking that the silly old fool would probably forget.

"Good, good," said the old man.

He served the food onto two plates and brought them to the table. He sat down opposite the Ranger and started to eat.

The two men ate in comfortable silence until the Ranger pushed his bread-polished plate from himself.

"That was delicious," he complimented the old man. "I can't remember the last time I had such a delicious meal."

"No I don't suppose you can," the old man replied as he stabbed at his last piece of bacon and popped it into his mouth.

I could, if I tried, thought the Ranger, but he had more important things on his mind other than having to remember the last delicious meal he'd eaten. He poured himself a mug of coffee and offered to pour some for the old man. The old man, his mouth full with the last remnants of his meal nodded. The Ranger poured the black, aromatic liquid. He took up his mug and leaned back into his chair. He lifted the mug and breathed in the strong aroma.

"This man you're looking for," the old man said around a mouthful of food, "what's he done?"

"Murder, rape, thievery, kidnap."

"My, he sounds like a nasty son of a gun. I guess I'm lucky to be alive."

The Ranger looked at him quizzically.

"Oh, I think he must have passed through here," the old man explained.

"When?"

"About a week ago, exactly a week ago, I reckon."

"What makes you think it was the man I'm after?"

The old man shrugged. "I don't get many visitors, as you can imagine. I have a few regulars; those that supply me with the things I can't grow. But he was in a rush, like you. He wanted to move on, not hang around. It was a shame, because I enjoyed his company. Like I'm enjoying yours."

The Ranger nodded. He took a sip of coffee. He was enjoying the old man's company. It seemed to be a while since he last enjoyed the companionship of a friendly man, even if he was a bit loopy.

"And I'm enjoying being here," he said. "I guess the man I'm after must have enjoyed your company as well, otherwise, I reckon, he would have killed you and then probably have strung your body up from some tree."

"That would have been difficult, "said the old man, "there's no trees round here."

The Ranger nodded. "It is pretty barren around here," he observed.

"It gets even worse in the direction you're going."

"How do you know that?"

"Because I know which way your man went. And it was straight into the desert. You really must have put the frighteners up him. I guess he reckons you'll not follow him into the desert. Maybe let him be?"

The Ranger shook his head. "I always get my man. Come hell or high water, I always get my man."

"So, you'll carry on?"

The Ranger looked at the old man. What sort of a dumb question was that to ask of a Texas Ranger?

"Yep," he said shortly.

"I thought so," said the old man. There was a note of sadness in his voice.

Poor lonely old bugger, the Ranger thought.

"I've no choice," he apologised. "The man has to be brought to justice."

"I know." The old man smiled unhappily. "In that case," he said in a more cheerful tone, "let's enjoy each other's company tonight." He stood up. "Come let's go sit somewhere more comfortable." He walked to a cupboard and extracted a bottle of bourbon and two glasses from it.

"That sounds like a grand idea," said the Ranger, standing up and following the old man out of the kitchen.

The two men entered the old man's sitting room. The lanterns hanging from the walls cast a warm, cosy glow around the orderly room.

"Sit," said the old man, "wherever you like."

The Ranger selected a comfortable looking bat-winged chair and settled into it. The old man placed the two glasses on a small table beside the Ranger and settled into a chair on the other side of it. He opened the bottle, poured the amber liquid and offered one glass to the Ranger.

"Your good health," the old man said, raising his glass.

"Likewise."

The Ranger took a sip and savoured the warming effects of the bourbon for a moment.

"You expecting a siege?" he asked drily.

The old man followed his gaze to a very large number of tins of beans and corned beef that were neatly stacked against a wall, from floor to ceiling, and some five rows deep. He chuckled.

"No, they're for emergencies. The winters can be pretty damned hard in this neck of the woods. There have been times when I've been snowed in for weeks on end."

"Looks like you could last more than a year with all those supplies."

"I reckon I might," chortled the old man. "But there's another reason for having them. I have a friend who visits me on a regular basis. We always have beans and corned beef when he visits. It's become a sort of habit of his. I like to think it will continue, even when I've passed from this world. Do you think that peculiar?"

The Ranger frowned. He did, but said, "Every man to his own."

*

The two men talked in amiable companionship, like two

old friends, for several hours. The bourbon slowly drained from the bottle and when the final drop was squeezed from it and had slid from his glass and down his throat, the Ranger declared it was time for him to hit the sack. He collected his kit and the old man showed him to his room.

"Would you like me to wake you in the morning?"

"No, thanks, I'll be fine."

"Well, good night, Seb."

"Good night, Robert."

The Ranger shut his door and grinned to himself. The crazy old coot was behaving like a parent. He removed his gun-belt, boots and outer clothes. He took his Colt from its holster and slipped it under the soft, down pillow. He climbed into the bed and relished the comfort of the horse-hair mattress. He snuggled under the crisp, clean bedding and fell asleep the moment his eyelids closed.

ONE

The Ranger woke with a start and drew his gun quickly from under the pillow. Sunlight cut a bright line between the closed curtains. Damn, he thought, I've overslept. I've never done that before, well not for years, and certainly not since I've been a Texas Ranger, which had been for longer than he cared to remember. He got out of bed and drew open the curtains. The room was at the back of the house and the window looked across the vegetable gardens and the maize crop, and on up the slopes of the ragged hill down which he had ridden the previous day. The sun was well above the top of the hill. Damn he really *had* overslept! Irritated with himself, he dressed quickly and strode through the house towards the smell of cooking.

"Good morning," the old man chirped, as he entered the kitchen.

"Morning."

"I've got a bath ready for you, out back, and sorted some clean clothes for you, from your kit. I've laid them on a chair beside the tub."

The Ranger raised his eyebrows in surprise.

"And I've packed your saddle bags with some supplies; beans, coffee and jerky; given you some oats for your horse and replenished your water. Oh, and I've tied two bundles of firewood for you. As you can imagine, there's none in the desert. It should last you four or five days, if you're sparing with it; that should be enough to get you across the desert."

"There was no ..."

The old man waved a hand.

"It's my pleasure. I always have more than I need."

"I'll pay for it, of course."

The old man turned to him.

"You got any money?" he asked.

The tone of his voice suggested that he already knew the answer.

"Well, no," replied the Ranger. Embarrassment prickled

his cheeks. "But," he continued quickly, "I'll send it on to you once I get to a town."

"Good idea, I'll write you an invoice. Now go have that bath, while I finish our breakfast."

The Ranger hesitated. He really needed to be getting going. But the trail ahead, into the desert, was going to be difficult, and dusty. He was pretty grimy as it was. He walked silently out of the door onto the veranda, and stripped.

*

"Your man went that way," said the old man pointing directly ahead from his front veranda. "I reckon the desert winds will have pretty much obliterated his tracks, but if you carry straight on, I reckon you'll come across the first camp he made after leaving me."

The Ranger squinted into the shimmering landscape. He stepped out of the shadows of the veranda canopy and climbed onto his horse.

"Well, thank you, Robert. I sure appreciate all your generosity."

"It was my pleasure, Seb."

Then the old man stepped forward, stood beside the Ranger's horse, laid a hand on the bridle and looked up at the Ranger.

"That desert is a dangerous place, son," he observed. "Full of mountain lions, rattlers and the like. If the desert doesn't get you, they probably will."

The Ranger looked down at the old man. A grin spread across his face.

"I'll be careful, old man," he said cheerfully.

"You do that."

The Ranger pulled his horse round and tipped the brim of his hat. "Adios!" he said as he spurred his mount into a gallop.

"Adios!" the old man called after him.

*

The Ranger slipped from his horse and squatted beside the cold ashes of a long-dead camp fire. That it was long-extinguished was obvious. A week, Robert had said since the man had visited him; that was probably about right.

He looked around into the growing gloom of early evening. All was quiet. A soft wind blew across the sands, as it had done virtually all day. It was obvious there was no better place to camp down. He decided he might as well stay put and set up camp right where he was. It was as good a place as any. The open landscape gave little chance for anyone to sneak up on him, but things might be different in the dark of night. He noted with interest that the grey ash of the old campfire was surrounded by a circular bank of earth. He tilted his head in appreciation. The man he was chasing obviously knew what he was doing, and did not want the flames of his fire to be too obvious in the flat landscape.

He stood up and leg hobbled his horse and relieved it of his saddle, kit and the bundles of firewood. He emptied two handfuls of oats into his hat and placed it on the ground in front of his horse. After gathering a few pieces of wood and pulling a few tufts of bone-dry grass from the sandy desert he went back to the fire place. Not wanting to signal his presence too much, he strengthened the circular bank around the fire place by scooping more sand onto it. Although he did not believe the man he was chasing was likely to be in the area, it was best not to take any chances. He set the firewood in place, lit the fire with practised ease and stared into the flames while they caught. Once the wood was glowing with heat he gathered his cooking utensils, food and coffee and began to prepare his evening meal.

*

As the Ranger sipped at his post-dinner coffee his mind drifted back to his recent encounter with Robert. He grinned into his coffee. The crazy old buzzard had been right, he mused, although, he had started to doubt it, started to wonder why he had taken the old fool's word for where the camp would be. But the few wind-worn tracks he had seen had corroborated what Robert had said – ride straight on and you should come across his first camp. And so he had, and now here he was, drinking coffee brewed on a fire in the place that the old bugger had predicted would be there. But of course, why should he have expected it to be any different. The best way to cross a desert was to go straight across it and not to waste time dilly-dallying around, zig-zagging this way and that. And this desert was as flat as a pancake. There were not even any dunes to obstruct one's path. If it carried on like this he just needed to set a bearing on a particular peak on the horizon each day and head for it. At the current rate of progress he would be through the desert in two days, three at the most, he concluded.

After draining the last of the coffee, he dampened the fire a little by scattering sand over the flames and rolled his blanket around him. He briefly studied the ocean of stars above, and watched a few of them shooting across the sky before drifting off to sleep.

TWO

Aha! thought the Ranger, as he drew his mount to a halt. Bingo! He was in a good mood. It had been a good day's tracking and now, just as he was thinking of stopping for the night, he found himself beside another small, sand encircled fireplace. He vaulted from his saddle and squatted beside the ashes. He knew, before examining it closely, that it was old and cold – he would not have been able to make up much time in a single day. It would likely be a long process of small incremental gains on his quarry - he nevertheless took up a pinch of ash and rubbed it between his finger and thumb.

He stood up with a light heart and set about making his camp in the growing gloom. He was pleased with himself. It had been a good day of tracking. He had not been caught out by the tactics of the man he was following, not that it had been that difficult. He did, however, have to admit to himself that he had made a beginner's mistake in assuming what the man had done on one day he would do on the next. The man had not continued on a dead straight line, as he had assumed he would. There had been no definite change in direction, but his obsession with using a particular mountain peak, on the horizon, as a guide had caused him to miss the subtle shift the man had made by veering off to the right. Really, for someone of his experience, the error was unforgivable! He had had to backtrack until he relocated the wind-worn trail and then follow it properly – like the expert he was. This little episode was something he would keep to himself. It would not form part of the anecdotes told when next meeting up with the other Texas Rangers as they'd rib him mercilessly for such a schoolboy error. He grinned to himself – he could just see their reaction. It was, he supposed, quite amusing – in hindsight. But he had learnt from his mistake and was now back on track, ignoring everything that went on around him. He was once again completely focused on following the trail.

*

With his dinner completed, he lay on his elbow with a mug of good, strong coffee in his hand. He took a sip. It really was very good. He wondered where the old man had acquired it. What was his name? Richard, no, Robert? It did not matter, he would never see the crazy old coot again. He wished he had asked him where he had got his coffee from.

He tilted his mug up and savoured the last drop of coffee. He folded his blankets around himself and snuggled into them. A light breeze brushed over him. He looked up into the heavens. He managed to count half a dozen shooting stars before drifting off to sleep.

THREE

"Hmm," the Ranger hummed to himself.

Was he imagining it or *were* these ashes a little fresher than those of the previous two camps? It was difficult to tell, even for an experienced tracker such as himself. He had started very early that morning, maybe the man he was chasing had remained in the previous camp a little longer, started off a little later. It was encouraging, but the gain he had made on the man was probably nothing dramatic. He could carry on, take advantage of the small gain he might have made, but it was probably not substantial enough, and although he had had another good day of tracking the past three long days in the saddle had made him a little stiff.

Since the fireplace, with its surrounding circle of sand, was all prepared he decided to camp there for the night. He stood up from his examination of the fire and set about making camp.

Rummaging through his saddle bag for his beans and jerky, his fingers brushed against something hard at the bottom of the bag. He took hold of the square object and withdrew it from the depths of his bag. It was a tin. He took it over to the light of the fire. It was a tin of corned beef. How on earth …? Of course, the old man, Greggor, or whatever his name was, must have hidden it inside his bag as a special treat. He did like corned beef very much. He licked his lips in anticipation and strode back to his saddle bag to find something to open the tin with.

*

The Ranger sat back with a contented sigh. This was the life! The freedom of camping wherever you wanted, the sounds of the night, a cool refreshing breeze against his face, blowing away the heat and sweat of the day, and good, strong coffee. There was of course the serious side of why he was where he was. The pursuit of the murderous, soulless killer he was after. He shook his head. How could anyone be so gutless? The cowardice of the man was exemplified in his flight across the desert. He was determined to avoid being brought to justice. A smile crept across the Ranger's face. Well, Sonny Jim, I'm afraid you're out of luck, because I'm not going to stop until I see you hanging from the end of a rope.

He took the last mouthful of coffee, wrapped his blanket around himself and, with an image of the captured murderer hanging from some scaffold swirling around his mind, he drifted off to sleep.

FOUR

The Ranger stood up from examining the fireplace. For some reason this one seemed older than any that he had recently examined. He looked around. The scrubby vegetation glowed in the rays of the low sun. It could be that the fireplace had been disturbed by animals. The landscape had become more scrubby, less desert like and he had noticed low stunted woodland ahead clothing a low ridge of hills. With all this vegetation, there would be more wildlife around and their scurrying about and curiosity might explain the poor condition of the circle of sand around the fire. He frowned. He hoped he had not lost the gain he had made on the man the previous day. No use pining over it, he thought, as he walked to his horse to get his fire lighting kit. And the last few pieces of fire wood.

*

He sat crosslegged, watching his food cook. He wondered about the animals that were skulking around in the dark.

They did not worry him. What was it the old man had said? Something along the lines that the desert was full of dangerous things, like cougars and rattlers. The Ranger grunted. The silly old bugger. He had forgotten to mention the main danger he was facing – the man he was chasing. In his experience cougars and rattlers avoided people – they did not come looking for trouble, but murderous sons-of-bitches, like Garrett, were different. He was the personification of trouble. Everywhere he went he caused death and destruction and it was a well-known fact that trouble spawned trouble.

When the Ranger had first come across him, Garrett had already gathered a gang of murderous outlaws around him, killing and raping, almost, it seemed, at will. Well, they had been made to pay for their crimes. All except Garrett, that was. The cowardly bastard had made good his escape while all the others had fought like men, if you could call that kind of person a man. The Ranger scowled in disgust at the thought of them. But at least they were more men than Garrett would ever be. That man was as likely as not to shoot you in the back. The Ranger felt a little sensation creep up his back. He turned to stare into the darkness. Of course, Garrett was not there, but the Ranger dampened the fire nonetheless by tossing a little sand over it.

He finished his coffee, snuggled into his blanket and making sure his Colt was firmly gripped in his fist; he closed his eyes and slept.

FIVE

The Ranger pulled on his reins, perplexed. He scanned the tall mesquite scrubland that surrounded him. Garrett seemed to have taken advantage of the fact that he had left the desert and entered a more densely vegetated landscape. The Ranger had expected the tracking to become more difficult, but not so quickly. He was now having to concentrate a whole lot more. He had managed to keep track of the trail Garrett had left for a while, but now it seemed to have completely disappeared. He scoured the ground for any signs. He needed to find the trail quickly, as the light was fading fast. The trail definitely came to this point before it petered out. There were no signs on the ground, so he guided his horse to turn in a series of slow circles. With each rotation, he raised his examination of the greenery of the shrubs a foot higher. Once round. Twice. Thrice. There! He stopped his horse and guided it to a shrub. He bent down to the height of his knee and studied the snapped twigs. He sat up and twisted each way throwing quick glances at the vegetation. No, this had to be it. He heeled his mount and forced it on through the stand of mesquite. And there it was – the anticipated camp fire.

This time there was no ring of sand, there was no need; the camp site was well hidden by the low branches of the scrub. He slipped from his horse, with a sense of exhilaration. There were signs that Garrett had been here for a while, evidence that he had spent more than one night here. He squatted beside the smear of ash. Hmm? It still looked as though the fire was a good few days old, but if Garrett had stayed awhile he might have gained a day or two on the man. That was encouraging, very encouraging.

He gathered some wood from the surrounding area, built a frame for his fire and went to his horse and collected his gear. He weighted the bag of coffee in his hand and decided to have two mugs in celebration.

*

The Ranger lay with his shoulders resting on his saddle and a warm mug of coffee resting on his chest, held comfortably in one hand. He watched the leaves above shift gently across the star-spangled sky as a breeze brushed softly over them. He was satisfied. His was a good life. It had been a long, hard chase, but now he could see the end of it in sight. In a few days from now he would have Garrett in his hands. The job would be over and then he could, at last, return home. How he looked forward to that. And he *would* go home, because, he did not expect the coward, Garrett, to put up a fight. Once Garrett saw him, he would toss his gun to the ground and it would be all over; weeks, months, of tracking the villain would be over.

He relished the last mouthful of coffee and wriggled down his saddle, drawing his blanket up over his chest.

"William Garrett," he muttered to himself, "your days are numbered."

He shut his eyes and drifted off to sleep, a smile etched on his lips.

SIX

"At last!"

The Ranger dragged himself off his horse. He did not even bother to examine the ashes. He was too dog tired. He immediately started making camp.

*

The Ranger sat staring into the flames of the fire. He held his mug of coffee against his upper lip and savoured the aromas that rose from it. He had only allowed himself one mug of coffee tonight. He shook his head slowly in acknowledgement of the skills that William Garrett had displayed that day. The man had led him a right merry dance, using all sorts of trickery to hide his tracks - sudden changes in direction, riding across rocky areas and then doubling back. The terrain had also become difficult – it was now hilly and craggy. And William Garrett seemed to have taken full advantage of it. He had left trails all over the place. It was like the entire area was filled with hoof prints. And so the Ranger had lost the trail on a number of occasions and had had to retrace his steps on each occasion. All in all, it had been an exhausting and frustrating day's riding.

Had William Garrett realised how close he was to being captured? The Ranger frowned as he considered the question.

"Not likely," he said to himself.

William Garrett was just being sensible. He would have done the same if he was being trailed. This had been the first real opportunity for William Garrett to make it difficult for anyone trailing him. It was the obvious thing to for him to do.

"You might be a coward, William Garrett, but you're no fool."

He took a deep inhalation of the coffee aroma and drained the mug. He lay down and pulled the blanket over him. He drifted asleep to a distant, melancholic, yapping howl of a coyote.

SEVEN/ZERO

"Damn! Damn!"

The Ranger scanned the gilded landscape at a complete loss. He had spent hours looking for the trail, but the ground on this ridge was nothing more than rafts of solid rock interspersed with hard-baked, rock-strewn earth. He knew William Garrett had come this way. The question was which way had he gone? Holding a hand up to protect his eyes from the low sun, he let his gaze roam over the wider landscape, hoping for some inspiration. None came. He urged his horse further up the slope so that he could look in that direction. He crested the ridge and jolted in surprise.

Below him, at the base of the small hill, was a house – quite a substantial house. What madman would build a house in this god-forsaken place? And why? He shrugged. Every man to his own, he thought. He guided his horse down a trail towards the house. Beyond it the landscape stretched to the horizon, flat as a pancake. He rode past a stand of corn and a vegetable garden. He continued across the yard and drew his horse to a halt in front of the house. He watched an old man step out from under the shadows of the canopied veranda of the house.

"Howdy," the old man said.

There seemed to be a look of recognition in his bright blue eyes. The Ranger leaned forward in his saddle and scrutinised his ragged, old face.

"Do I know you?" he asked.

The old man looked at him for a moment, as though searching for something.

"I don't believe so," he replied, with an edge of resignation to his voice.

The Essence of War is Secrecy

Thomas Begley

"The essence of successful warfare is secrecy. The essence of successful journalism is publicity". So said the pamphlet issued to us by the Queen's Best, lazily slid over to me and narrowly missing a substantial pool of stagnating Fosters that the slider had spilt not ten minutes previously. This guy – let's call him Fosters – was the only reporter who had taken me up on the offer of a night-time jaunt through the cracked and faded streets of Olde Towne Portsmouth. I couldn't stand the thought of staying cooped up in my little hotel room on my last night of freedom.

You could feel the deep loneliness of these dockside pubs. The walls, windows and, most profoundly, the floorboards wept, rattled and creaked as they mourned the loss of their long-gone sea-loving clientele, replaced by red-skinned brummies dripping their sticky, limp 99 Flakes all over the scruffy, fag burned, deep maroon carpets. The kind of maroon which suggested a once vibrant scarlet, before years of milk stout, crisps and ash had been ground in by decades of negligence (much like that of our Fosters sloshing friend). I leafed through the pamphlet for want of something better to do, as the reporter adjacent to me drank down the last of his cheese and onion crisps, much of it tumbling into his scruffy mousy-brown beard. As I stared at the green paper, the words blurred into a black soup of incomprehensible nothingness. I began to wonder how well the British military usually took to groups of nagging journalists worming in and around their perfectly ordered ranks. Especially since we would all be sloshing around together in a little iron prison, the constant swell and tensions from the permanence of our proximity was bound to cause at least some frustration?

It seemed odd to me that the military would disallow experienced war reporters for this particular venture. I suppose I shouldn't really be complaining. This assignment did at least provide proper employment for me. I knew I didn't have the qualifications for real war reporting, but since they kicked off the fellas who did, I wasn't going to pass up the opportunity. I can see, though, if you were trying to cover your back, disallowing professional war reporters would make sense. Those guys know how to work the military mind, tricking even the most decorated officers into letting things slip. They really do know how to squeeze every last drop out of Her Majesty's finest rifle-touting oranges. But at least these journalists were experienced at this sort of thing; they would understand how the army lived and make sure they never really got in the way until they needed too – which, I'm sure, would make life a lot easier for all involved in such conditions. But I suppose they felt like they had to protect their own and, to be honest, I don't blame them.

"I bet you," Fosters mumbled loudly, spraying the already beer-soaked table with the last of his crisp crumbs, the whole thing, by this point, looking more like a marshy waterscape than an Edwardian wooden dining table. "I bet you, that this crisis will be resolved before the end of the month… five quid!"

To be honest with you, I wouldn't have put the end date much later than that. My estimations were that, our ship at least, would dock for a couple of weeks on Ascension Island, showing just enough of a threat and readiness to war if the need truly arose, giving the big wigs in London, Washington, Buenos Aires and the UN enough time to wrestle out some sort of diplomatic solution. So I placed my bet ten days into May and we shook on it.

*

"Don't cry for me Argentina, we're going to knock the shit out of you." These words plastered over the ample bosoms of two young well-wishers, screaming and waving the red, white and blue as we stood, looking over them, on the main deck of the Canberra waiting to cast off. In the foreground, the brass band was bawling out "Land of Hope and Glory", and the Union Jacks seemed to flap and bob to the tune. The whole affair would have looked far more fitting if viewed from a 1940s news reel. If we're being frank, it all seemed a bit over the top, serenading a Falklands war that was unlikely to occur.

Whilst I stood enjoying the patriotic festivities below, Fosters slid beside me and gave me a nudge. I noticed he had shaved since our little outing the night before, and under the scruffy curls of his chin there was a fairly handsome face. He had a distinctly dimpled chin, which looked quite becoming on him. He informed me that the Senior Naval Officer, Captain Burne, had made it quite clear that stowing journalists was the least of his priorities on the Canberra, so they put us on one of the lower cockroach-infested decks. 'Typical,' I thought. If the relationship between us and the forces was going to stay like this, I wasn't sure if any worthwhile information was going to be gleaned from this job at all. As we were talking about the situation we two journalists had found ourselves in, there came a distinct jolt from the hull of the ship. We both looked at each other and knew that we had just begun the longest and most arduous cruise we would ever have the pleasure of being on.

*

I was sat in my cabin. It had been around two weeks since the patriotic Portsmouth send-off, and I had just about gotten used to life at sea. The constant swell of the Atlantic no longer sent my head spinning, so I could now walk in a straight line no matter how heavy the waves. My digs were uncomfortable. The steel walls, covered in flaking avocado green paint, matched the colour of the water, which completely eclipsed the small porthole on a permanent basis. This forced me to keep the fluorescent tube bulb that dominated the 5.9-foot-high ceiling almost permanently ablaze, giving everything a 'peaky' appearance, as though the room itself was getting ill from the rolling ocean. Surprisingly, the cockroaches kept their distance, and at the desk sat my IBM Selectric II and a mug of often stale tea.

On Easter Sunday we had our first press conference. The ship's staff led us into one of the ship's cinema rooms. There were 14 of us altogether, and we were left to sit where we may. I decided it would be best to keep away from the rest of the bunch as much as possible. I never even much liked journalists, or 'Hacks' as the military affectionately called us. On the whole, we were a narcissistic bunch, who only really enjoyed each other's company when there was something to gain from it. I spotted Fosters's auburn locks close to the front of the cinema but thought better of relocating next to him. He had proven himself an exception to my journalistic aversion – I really did enjoy his company.

The lack of natural light in this room gave it a mysterious lustre; the dusty velvet curtains surrounding the screen, the musty smell and worn out leather seating added to this. We were left waiting nearly fifteen minutes before the ship's captain, Dennis Scott-Masson, arrived, which gave me enough time to clean my fingernails and fish out some worryingly hard wax from my ears. Captain Scott-Masson was a fairly well-groomed and shy man. Evidently not used to talking with the press, he made sure that we all knew he was under orders from the MoD and so wouldn't take any messing around. Evidently, he was very conscious of his position as a citizenry captain, and did not want anyone to take advantage of this fact. After avoiding some questions about the ship's capacity to hold so many heavily active military personnel, we were all dismissed. Being none the wiser than when we entered the conference, I decided to take a stroll to the canteen area where there was a nice panoramic view of the ship's main decks.

I sat down at one of the large windows with a cup of tea and began thinking about how I would frame my second piece to send back to London. By this point, it had become obvious that any information we produced whilst working with the MoD would have to reflect positively on the forces or it would never get past the censors. The information and press policy on this particular ship had been a mess from the offset. This policy came from four highly uncoordinated sources: the MoD, Fleet HQ of the Royal Navy at Northwood, the Task Force Commander and the Senior Naval Officer Captain Burne. The poor sods that policed these policies – the "Brain Police" or the MoD press office as they were officially called – had the trust of neither the press nor the military, living in an uncomfortable no-man's-land between the two.

These folks were young, though with some journalistic training, and had no experience with the kind of "big press" stories that we were running. I was chatting to one of them when trying to get my first story out via the Marine satellite (Marisat); he let slip that they weren't even trained in censorship, that the military hadn't even given them that. These folks had no chance. Their confusion was evident from the first time Fosters and I stepped foot into their office where the Marisat was located. Both our reports were mainly focused on the living conditions of the armed forces aboard the Canberra, and Fosters' was sent off without any trial. However, when it came to my piece, the use of the word Canberra was instantly flagged up and censored. With no explanation of why, in a matter of fifteen minutes, the name of the ship was no longer acceptable to report, and I was sent out of the door, my report well on its way to London with obvious blank spots.

*

By the time the Canberra had left the Ascension Islands, the canteen seat in front of the large windows had become my regular musing and writing spot. The shiny hard plastic of the high stool stopped me from ever becoming too comfortable, meaning that I never fell into thoughts of a comfortable and useless nature – it kept me alert; alertness being something fairly hard to achieve when living on a ship for so long. The constant roll of the hull and the fairly sedentary lifestyle certainly encouraged a sluggish and languishing mind. Luckily, the tea supply was almost constant, and tea, as many a drinker knows, allows for lubrication of thought. It was nearly a month since we had set off from Portsmouth, and my bet with Fosters regarding the end of the crisis was looking like a sure win – not that I was particularly happy with the looming reality that a diplomatic solution may not be reached.

As I peered out of the slightly foggy windows at the sun-drenched deck below, I could see the 3rd Battalion, Parachute Regiment sprinting, twisting, jumping and squirming through all of the obstacles the architecture of the ship could supply. The whole operation looked like a unified parasite gnawing and sucking at the Canberra, sussing out ways in which to devour the great animal. Evidently the unit was tight; they were fluid and uniformed together, achieving far more as a team than they ever could as individuals.

In many respects, we as reporters were in polar opposition. We never trusted each other. Even when we were together, we would keep our distance, scratching and scraping at our subjects for any information that would put us ahead of the game; climbing the constantly overpopulated ladder that was the media, kicking, punching and scheming our way to the non-existent top. It's no surprise that our slippery nature often led to poor relations with our subjects, which definitely included the military aboard the Canberra. In the same vein, however, there was a sense from the servicemen that their job was just naturally more important than ours, which was bound to get our backs up. Distrust was the name of the game between us. Though, at least, they had each other to rely on.

I noticed something whilst still peering out of that window. Hidden between the scores of ultra-fit military personnel were slobby, hacking and wheezing civilians. These journalists were running and jumping to keep up with the real athletes. At this point, I realised something, something that made me feel both uncomfortable and warmed. We journalists envied the soldiers! Maybe not their dogmatic approach to life, nor their single-minded schoolboy ways, but it was the pride within themselves, their dedication to their comrades and their duty. These are the elements that the press naturally do not harbour – it would be counter-productive to our profession. But seeing these men exercising, following the orders of an ancient patriarchal regime, you could see their desire for something more – for the camaraderie that was simply not present in their normal existence.

I suddenly felt deeply alone. Sat in the cold canteen, looking down upon the activities below, I wanted to be a part of this – to feel a part of something bigger, to be dependent and depended upon. I leapt up from my plastic throne, threw back the last of my now cold tea and made my way down to the main deck of the ship. My legs were moving faster than my mind could understand, and I nearly tripped on the cold metal steps of the service stairwell. I could see the door to the main deck through the small frosty window. There was a flurry of movement, and by this point I was sprinting. It hadn't occurred to me that I may have to stop before opening the door and, in seconds, my face had collided with the bolted steel frame of its window. With my left cheek throbbing, I threw open the door, feeling the rush of refreshing yet surprisingly warm air surround me.

At this very moment, I could see first-hand the change in the relationship between "us and them". Journalists being wailed at by the command, hands slapping the backs of lagging joggers as they were lapped for the umpteenth time. Suddenly, it seemed, we had respect for the military other, and by the looks of things, we were trying to gain theirs by showing our ability to muck in. As I stood watching and assessing this new situation, Fosters came panting from around the starboard side of the ship. He smiled groggily and stopped by me to take a breather. "You fancy a go?" he wheezed, grimacing and sucking in air like a man possessed.

In all honesty, I was a little bit nervous to try and run with the 'best of them'; my fitness hadn't been tested since Kingston Grammar's sports day 1970. But before I could really make up my mind, a burly commando came bounding round the corner, and grabbing my arm, he bellowed, "C'mon lad, let's see what you can do!"

And with that, I was whisked away into a world of sweat, burning lungs and torn ligaments.

The sea was particularly heavy that evening. I was sat in my room, nursing my raw knee and inspecting the large bruise that had developed across my left cheek in a tiny compact mirror. A fly was clinking and buzzing at the fluorescent lightbulb blazing overhead, and the cockroach infestation had definitely grown in severity (I had found three of the buggers writhing over each other at the end of my left trainer, which was less than pleasant). But regardless of the pathetic position I found myself in, I was in very good humour. For the first time aboard the Canberra, I felt welcome. The extensive fitness regime had been hard, but I relished the constant jibs and jibes from the commandos as I struggled round the decks of the ship. Finally, I felt a sense of unity between both breeds of men, and I hope that they felt the same.

It didn't take us journalists long to become what I like to call "troopy groupies". The raw masculinity of the men gave, at least me, a kind of schoolgirl admiration for them, like a teenager at a Beatles concert, though I fear if I had tried to pull even a single hair from their heads, I would no longer have a finger to call my own. Unlike the soldiers, I had a personal radio at my disposal, and whatever information I could glean from London would be quickly relayed to the men in a desperate attempt to try and win over their trust and respect (which I'm sure made me seem like teacher's pet, leaving apple after apple on their desks). But for this, I think some respect was reciprocated. We were the closest things these noble warriors had to newspapers, and for that, at least, they seemed appreciative.

*

As I was walking along towards the shower rooms on the fourth of May, my wash bag swung from a long thin piece of rope wrapped between my fingers. With only a towel between my bare bottom and the dank chilly air, I shivered. The cold steel against my feet made me curse that I had not worn some sort of footwear. Whilst I walked hunched against the cold, trying desperately to control the shivers that were quickly rising up inside me, Fosters came flying down the corridor.

"Have you heard the news!?" he fumbled out of his overly excited lips.

In truth, I hadn't, but I was soon to be told. Fosters put his arm over my shoulder and led me back to my room, much to my protest. My towel was rather short, and when sat on the bed I had a hard time of keeping my modesty. But he didn't seem to notice. He sat uncomfortably close to me and began to relay the news.

Apparently the Argentine forces had sunk the HMS Sheffield, only two days after the Belgrano. The motive for this sinking was obvious: RETALIATION! This I needed to report, and quickly! I couldn't be the last journalist to get this news to London. Forgetting my shower (and the presence of Fosters), I shot up. Losing my towel in my excitement, I scrabbled around relocating and reapplying my clothes. Before you could say Belgrano, I was speeding down the hallway with my notepad and pen. Fosters wasn't far behind. We had become very comfortable around the soldiers by this point, a mistake that would all too soon be realised.

Within a matter of minutes, I found myself sat in my usual plastic stool. In my excitement I had forgotten even my usual cup of tea, so I certainly hadn't noticed the abundance of very sombre looking officers surrounding me. With a dedicated smirk on my face I began frantically writing all of the information I had from Fosters, embellishing the information when needed (as is journalistic custom).

As I wrote, the feeling of being watched grew stronger and stronger, like a dozen burning-hot pokers at the back of my skull. As my writing slowed I felt the tight grip of a strong, rough hand pulling at my shoulder, each finger sending blasts of icy cold fear down my spine. Before I knew it, the small of my back was pushed hard against the desk I was writing at only a second before. I was face to face with a group of disgusted and very angry soldiers, the broadest of which now had his nose a quarter of an inch away from mine. I could smell the baked beans on his breath and could see, very clearly, the blackheads speckling the top of his eyebrows.

"If you don't very quickly find at least an ounce of respect in that podgy little Hack body of yours," he loudly whispered through gritted teeth, "me and the rest of the boys will be happy to introduce you to little Miss Atlantic out there. I've heard she's quite fond of spineless, book-loving boys such as yourself."

I was too afraid to say anything, but we all knew I understood what he was trying to say. I had overstepped the mark with my excitement. I had not even begun to contemplate the real world effects of the sinking of the HMS Sheffield. He let me go and I sat down. I still desperately needed to finish this article very much against the wishes of the military.

I slowly made my way back to my room. All the men in the canteen were well aware of what I was about to do. I was about to benefit from the news that many of their fellow soldiers may have died, that British women and children had lost their fathers, uncles and sons. They wanted to keep this quiet, to allow themselves time to digest the tragedy that had happened so recently, to allow the families just a little privacy before the press' slimy fingers got hold of the information. It's what the men and their families at the very least deserved. But I knew very well that I wasn't going to respect this and, worst of all, I was going to benefit from it. Alas, this is the nature of my work, and that is the nature of theirs. This is when I finally realised that we would never truly get on; the best we could do was tolerate one another to keep face until the whole affair was finally over.

Sources:

Barnes, J. (2002). *The worst reported war since the Crimean.* Available: http://www.theguardian.com/media/2002/feb/25/broadcasting.falklands. Last accessed 28/03/2016.

Badsey, S. Havers, R. Grove, M (2005). *The Falklands Conflict Twenty Years on.* Abingdon: Frank Cass. pp. 39-42.

Rai, A, K. (no date). *Media at War: Issues and Limitations.* Available: http://www.idsa-india.org/an-dec-00-6.html. Last accessed 29/03/2016.

Gibran, D, K (1998). *The Falklands War: Britain versus the past in the south Atlantic.* Jefferson: McFarland & company. pp.17-19.

Fox, R (1982). *Eyewitness Falklands.* London: Methuen. pp.1-4-5-9-10-82.

Vine, A (2012). A Very Strange Way to Go to War: The Canberra in the Falklands. London: Aurum Press Ltd. pp.62-64.

The Perfect Murder
(in Nine Easy Steps)
Matthew Coburn

'You are through to the Wilson family. Sorry we're out. Leave a message…'

Oh damn. It's that chirpy answerphone message. Then it comes to life.

"Hello, who is it?"

"Oh, hi Steve, it's me."

"Hello, Uncle Jack, it's James."

"I'm sorry. Don't you sound like your Dad? Whoops. I guess that's the last thing you want to hear. Teenagers sounding like their parents. What could be worse? You'll be listening to seventies music next. It's about time he introduced you to some Led Zeppelin."

"Ha, I would rather eat broccoli… I'll just go and tell Dad it's you."

The phone-line goes quiet as James looks for his Dad in the garage, or the garden shed, or perhaps even the hammock. James is a good lad. He is the eldest son of my brother (and colleague) Mr Steve Wilson QC.

Steve seems to have it all. Like me, he is a successful small-town lawyer, but he has so much more. He has a happy marriage and teenage kids. At least his marriage seems happy enough, and Mary is gorgeous… for forty-

231

something. He gets the best corporate cases and I get the alimony jobs. He gets the libel, with all the case law to consider, while I get the social-benefits fraud. After our father died, his will specified that the company name would change from 'Wilson and Son' to 'Wilson and Co'. Why not 'Wilson Bros' or 'Wilson and Wilson'? Dad never accepted me failing my barrister exams.

Anyway, it's not for much longer. Soon, no more of the purgatory of looking after Mum. No more playing second-fiddle to Steve Wilson, Barrister at Law. Along with the string of failed relationships and one-night stands, these will soon all be far behind me.

A week ago, brother Steve agreed to look after that package for me.

"It's a present for Mum," I said. "I can't hide it in our tiny flat, because her annoying little terrier will sniff it out. Even with dementia Mum will find it. You know I got rid of the car after my ban, so I have nowhere to put it. Don't tell anybody about it. Not Mary, or the kids. Especially the kids. You know what chatterboxes they are. You promise."

Poor Mum has gone downhill tragically fast. These days she spends her time looking around to see if anything has moved since yesterday. She doesn't even recognise me anymore. Steve agreed to put the package in his garage until Mum's birthday, which is next week. He complained that his dog Arthur won't stop sniffing it and barking at it.

"What's in that package? Arthur's going mental around

it. I've had to shut him out the back of the house all week," Steve protested the last time I rang.

Oh dear, poor Arthur. Steve could shut him in the tennis court, or else he can play in the swimming pool. Still, it's not ideal. I should have double-wrapped or even triple-wrapped that package in more plastic bags. I couldn't smell anything once I put the clothes in that heavy-duty bin liner. Steve didn't say anything about a smell, but dogs have that super-sense. Who would have thought that a tramp could smell that bad?

"What do you think it is?" I said, "...a bag of clothes to disguise Mum's body!" I continued with a fake laugh. "We all have our little secrets, don't we?"

My darling big brother knows that I know about his affair. He also knows that Mary has better lawyers than either of us. Her father is none-other than Judge Kline, formerly of 'Kline, Kline and Co'. They are proper, big-city lawyers. I joked about disguising Mum's body on a whim, but it might also prove useful to rope him into my plan indirectly.

"Anyway," I continued, "Mum deserves a treat, and she got quite excited when I mentioned a birthday party for her next week."

So, the package 'for Mum's birthday' found its way into Steve's garage. The hurried wrapping is my fault. Drunk at the time - some would say 'pissed out of my head' - I tell myself the booze made me do it. It certainly made me so desperate for a pee that I stumbled into the bushes down by the river. Being so drunk at least made me oblivious to the smell. It MUST have been the alcohol that made me think I could get away with taking the clothes from that dead tramp and pushing her body into the river.

I don't know what gave me the idea of using the tramp's clothes to disguise Mum's body one day, and obviously no-one would miss that destitute old woman. Not much more than bones lay there, so her body-parts will never be found in that fast flowing, swamp-like, suburban drain.

Now, I wait for Steve to come to the phone, with my mind wandering off on murderous fantasies. Idly chewing the corner of my mobile phone, it springs into action. I don't catch the first part of the belated reply, but I hear the second part.

"I'll kill that bloody dog. Get it out of the kitchen. Oh no, not the fish tank!"

"Steve. Steve?" I manage to say, just as he disappears to sort out the dog.

I resume my recollections of that fateful night down by the river a week ago - going over the plan in my head one more time.

Step One is already complete. I have taken the tramp's clothes and left them at Steve's, as a present for Mum.

Step Two: I invite everybody to a big party for Mum's birthday next week. That will show how caring I am.

Step Three: I arrange a little accident for Mum, when the time is right. Everybody knows it would be an act of kindness to let her go. It's just that no-one will say it.

Step Four: I get the package and dress her as the tramp lady, before leaving her down by the river. A brilliant way to dispose of the body. Mum is skin and bone these days anyway, and they won't find her for a while even if they get lucky.

Step Five: Then I go away for the weekend before Mum's party, to establish a cast-iron alibi. The care agency can be booked to do the chores, and everybody knows I need a break.

All these steps are making even me think that I am a bit obsessive compulsive. "Kids. Go and peel Uncle Jack a grape," Steve would say at family get-togethers. He thinks he's so funny, joking about some of my little habits.

Step Six: The agency will call me in Paris, when they get no answer from Mum. I call her from my hotel and obviously get no answer - then I report her missing to the police.

Step Seven: If, or more likely when, they find Mum's body during the search, it will be dressed like the old tramp-lady and mistaken for her. I might have to rough her up a bit first and swap the wedding rings. Dad wouldn't mind, if it means that he sees Mum in the hereafter a bit sooner than expected.

Step Eight: The masterpiece! The local constabulary will investigate the wrong death. There is no need for expensive DNA or time-consuming dental-records in a simple 'misadventure' case.

Step Nine: My dear, missing, demented Mum will simply never be found.

The perfect murder - except it is a mercy killing. An old tramp dies and an old woman goes missing. No one will link the two, as long as the smelly package of clothes remains a secret. Why should even Steve, the brilliant lawyer, tell the police about a birthday present kept in his garage. He wouldn't risk suggesting a connection to his mother's disappearance? Even if suspicion got the better of him, he wouldn't sacrifice his oh-so-perfect lifestyle to get justice for our dear mother, not without hard evidence anyway.

I try to imagine him being interviewed by the police, to help them find Mum.

It might go like this… "Well, Officer, now you mention it… my brother did say he would use the package of clothes in my garage to disguise Mum's body." Hardly credible, and more likely to get him arrested. Not forgetting I know about his affair. He hasn't helped Mum at all since her memory failed. Not once has he come round and put the dinner on, or helped with the chores. As long as Mum is someone else's problem, he is happy, especially since the dementia got really bad.

"Is anybody there?" I say into my mobile in a rising, sarcastic tone.

Steve has one of these roaming house-phones, so I am probably perched on the sideboard in the kitchen, talking to the bread bin.

"Hello. Brother Jack here." I vainly try again. It's amazing how the seconds pass so slowly, while their 'quality family time' no doubt rushes by. Mary loves to say how time flies. Well actually, no it doesn't. Life drags itself from one grinding day into another and then you die. At least, with Mum gone, I can sell the house and disappear to Thailand, or somewhere like that.

While I wait forever for Steve to come back to the phone, my mind goes back to my plan. Step one is done: the tramp has been washed away and her clothes are in Steve's garage as a secret birthday present for Mum next week. Step two: I sent the party invites out to everybody yesterday. Step three: Mum had her little accident this morning, with a pillow. She always said "If I get that bad, then let me go." Now step four – the big one: I take Mum's body to the river and dress her in the tramp's clothes. I just need the package from Steve. How hard can that be? That damn dog.

My mobile jumps to life again, with the sound of crashing and banging on the other end of the line.

"Steve, I haven't got forever. I need to catch a flight to

Paris. The agency has the details and they will look after Mum for a couple of days."

"Just a minute. I'll be right back!" I catch the essence of the garbled message from the other end of the call.

I mustn't forget to get rid of Mum's dog. Who in their right mind would give up their freedom for a dog? People with kids I guess, since they have no freedom anyway. It's worse than being a prisoner of war when the babies arrive: no sleep, stress positions, 'white' noise all the time, shit everywhere. Having kids would be illegal under the Geneva Convention.

If I didn't live in a flat with Mum, I could have kept the package of clothes myself. If I had a garage, never mind a triple-garage like Steve, I could have stored it there: but I don't. If I thought Steve's 'oh-so-pure-bred' hound would try to get to the package, then I would have stuck it under a bush somewhere. Then what if some other mangy canine had got to it and ripped it apart?

At last my mobile communicates again. I can hear barking in the background and the sound of my niece shouting at Arthur to go into the garden. They have a garden like Hampton Court Palace, so if I lived there that damn dog would never be allowed into the house. Why can't they just chain it to the kennel like normal people do? The shouting from my niece is so loud that I hold my mobile at arm's length. Now I have the speaker away from my ear, but the mouthpiece is also out of range. Above the barking of the dog, contact is being offered from Steve's end, at last.

"Hello, are you still there? Don't hang up." Some sanity seems to have been restored at the Wilson household.

"Shut that damn dog up," I shout down the length of my arm.

A door slams at the other end and some peace settles over cyberspace.

"Hellooooo. Are you still there?" A plea finally comes from the other end.

I briefly scorn the family photo on my mobile screen. Mum and I, Steve, Mary, and the kids, all staring tight-lipped at the camera at Dad's funeral. Then I pull the phone to my chin and launch into a tirade, which even as I chunter away, I think I may regret for the rest of my life.

"Steve, I need that package right now," I said. "It's very important that I have it before Mum's birthday party, before I go to Paris. You'd better still have it. You swore. 'I will keep your little secret,' you said. 'Just be careful with MY little secret,' you said. I have never asked a lot from you, so if you have told anybody about that package… well, I just don't know. Perhaps those blue pills that you get delivered to Mum's house… they will have to go to your address instead of ours."

"Sorry Uncle Jack, it's still James here. What package? What pills? How's Gran?"

*

Only two days later I'm back from Paris, much earlier than planned.

I had finally spoken to Steve and he had brought the 'birthday' package round to our office. He didn't suspect a thing, as he is so caught up in his own wonderful life. I'd given him the little sachet of blue pills as usual. I had not been able to resist a little nod toward his pretty secretary and a sarcastic comment... 'I hope you two have fun with these,' I'd said with a wink.

Step four had gone well. Disposing of the body is always the hardest part, but I took poor, lifeless Mum to the river, rolled her around in the dirt, and dressed her as the tramp, as planned. The wedding ring fitted perfectly. No doubt Mum is blessing me from heaven for bringing an end to her torment. I think she would have been proud of my foolproof strategy.

Then with nearly everything going to plan, step five needed slight amendment. After booking the care agency for Mum, I packed my bag for Paris. I just had to take a little detour. Unexpectedly, I had to go around to Steve's first, because of that little hitch - James had heard me ranting about the secret package.

Step six went perfectly. The agency called me when they got no answer from Mum. I called her vainly and reported her missing to the police.

I am now back early from my trip, after only one night in that romantic city. Not only is Mum missing, but something really terrible has happened.

James went missing too. Very out-of-character, but perhaps he went looking for Gran. It turns out he had an accident in the swimming pool. Drowned under the pool covers. Shame about that. Nice lad.

Contributors' Biographies

Steven Battersby spent his childhood in the hilly countryside of Surrey, within easy reach of the Sussex coast, before moving to West Oxfordshire. This is his first published writing. For his day-job he is a Design Engineer in the Broadcast Industry. His interests include music and ancient history, and one day, given the chance, he would like to sail on a Viking Longship.

Thomas Begley recently graduated from Keele University with an honours degree in Politics. Since then, he has been flitting between his home village in rural west Oxfordshire and the equally rural town of De Pere, Wisconsin (USA). Currently in pursuit of a career in radio, he spends his time boating in the idyllic Wisconsin north woods and tinkering with motor vehicles. This will be Tommy's first published work, with the hopes of more to come.

Matt Coburn was born into the Royal Air Force, and spent much of his childhood living out of a suitcase. He now lives in Oxfordshire, where he enjoys painting, cycling, wine, beer and pickles. He has self-published a novel (under a pseudonym) about girl-power in stone age North America. He has also published several short stories in local anthologies.

David Lawrence was born in Rugby, worked in

Publishing, spending 15 years as Production Director before taking early retirement in 2007. He has always written for pleasure and has a poetry blog under the name *divalde*. Interests include music (rock and jazz), history, walking and reading. He is a regular visitor to the Bodleian Library and is a Friend of the Ashmolean Museum in Oxford.

David Lloyd is a former newspaper journalist and magazine editor. He has also worked in marketing, public relations and fundraising across the charity sector, and has a passion for editing anything that other people write. He lived in the Middle East before moving to Oxfordshire. Interests include making cocktails, motorbikes (from a distance), wines and writing. His quizzes are famous, at least within his family. He would like to add 'keeping fit' to his list of interests but his children know otherwise.

Martin Marais was born in Zambia and spent much of his childhood in South Africa, but now lives in Oxfordshire. He has published several novels, including a military history novel set in the Anglo-Boer War and a number of Westerns (as Martyn C Marais). He has also published several short stories. When not writing, Martin enjoys reading, walking, cycling, photography and the red wines of South Africa and South America.

Lucy McGregor grew up in West Oxfordshire; she tried to move away a couple of times, but it didn't take. She designs roads and sewers for a living and writes for fun, alongside archery, church bell ringing, pen-and-paper role-playing games, and increasingly ambitious DIY home improvements. Be cautious if approaching unreasonably early in the day (before about lunchtime) and avoid her cooking.

Rhonda Neal was born in south London but has lived more of her life in Oxfordshire. She has had a career as a physiotherapist in the NHS. She is now pursuing her interests in all things creative. This is her first short story to be published, and hopefully not the last.

Khadija Rouf was born in Liverpool and now lives in Oxfordshire. She is a keen writer and has published poetry, and a children's book, *Gloria Exbat*.

Jackie Vickers has had many different and interesting occupations but now prefers to escape into imaginary worlds of her own making.

Stephen Young has always, for as long as he can remember, anyway, written for fun. This is his first published short story. In his spare time, he enjoys cooking, travelling and early twentieth century weird fiction.

Printed in Great Britain
by Amazon

20110517R10144